Save Our Shop

Save Our Shop

William Bridge Mysteries Book 1

Michael N. Wilton

Contents

Chapter One: A Very Frustrated Helper . . 1

Chapter Two: A Proper Job 18

Chapter Three: Word Gets Around 39

Chapter Four: Big Business Moves In . . . 63

Chapter Five: The Break-in 82

Chapter Six: Help Is At Hand 103

Chapter Seven: The Get Together 129

Chapter Eight: Up Against It 148

Chapter Nine: Lady C Hits Back 167

Chapter Ten: William Has an Idea 192

Chapter Eleven: Thrashing It Out 207

Chapter Twelve: Ed's Arsenal 222

Chapter Thirteen: Sneaking In 240

Chapter Fourteen: Getting the Goat 258

Chapter Fifteen: Panic Stations 278

Chapter Sixteen: Hands Off 295

Chapter Seventeen: A Case of Mistaken
    Identity 311

Chapter Eighteen: Equal Rights 323

About The Author 339

Chapter One
A Very Frustrated Helper

In the picturesque village of Snuggleton-near-the-Sea, the afternoon was drawing to a close at the end of a hot summer's day. The sun still shone on the few remaining villagers taking a stroll before supper, and everywhere seemed peaceful and serene – except for a time bomb about to go off in the village shop halfway down the High Street.

Inside, Mavis Foxey was fuming. With every passing minute she was becoming increasingly annoyed at her missed opportunities. All afternoon she had been doing her best to attract the manager, Albert Bridge, and get him involved in a full blown scandal, and any moment he would be asking her to bring in the display boards, signalling the end of another day.

Her pride depended on it. In her view, it was time for immediate action. The thought of what Fred – or Foxy Fred, as her husband was known - would say if she failed him, when his whole ambitious building scheme depended on it, sent a cold tremor down her spine. It wasn't the only reason, of course – if she pulled it off she stood to win a substantial bet with her friend, Enid. She smirked to herself. That was something she'd never had any trouble with before, as most of the men in the village would testify to their cost.

Aware the time was slipping by she attacked the keyboard with renewed fury and was gratified to see she had hit the jackpot. Immediately, a total of £9,999 flashed up. That should do the trick, she decided. Taking a quick look around, she carelessly undid the top three buttons of her blouse and shook her hair free.

"Oh dear, I don't think this till likes me," said Mavis raising her voice, as she checked the total. "That can't be right, what do you think, Mr Bridge?" she called out and as he reluctantly came up to see what was wrong, she brushed against him as if by accident.

It was coming up to five-thirty and all Albert Bridge wanted to do was to shut up shop and get home to his supper. It had been a long day and he was tired. The bread had come in late and the greengrocery order was up the creek; his usual assistant, Jackie, who did all the ordering, was away sick, and the temp they were promised hadn't turned up. The last thing he wanted to do was to get involved with an old biddy like Mavis.

Normally a friendly and trusting person, Albert was reaching the end of his tether. Usually, he was never short of female help when he needed it, especially from some of the more elderly spinsters who were always looking in for an excuse to linger. But it was holiday time and there was scarcely a soul around –except Mavis. He didn't mind giving a pat of encouragement to some of the locals who helped to keep the village shop going – but he had to draw a line somewhere. His long suffering friend, Hettie, always smiled patiently when Mavis's name was mentioned, saying the old 'man-eater' had a face that would stop a bus a mile away. Although he was always ready to defer to her better judgement where such matters were concerned, on this occasion he thought she was underestimating – two miles, more likely. He backed away hastily, avoiding the open invitation.

"Why don't you finish off and go home, Mavis – I'll sort it out," he said hastily. "I expect your husband will be home by now, wanting his supper. We don't want to keep him waiting, do we?" he added heartily.

"But just look at this figure." Adding emphasis, she tugged at her blouse, and leaned forward provocatively. "I don't like the look of it, do you?"

"No, I can't say I do," he agreed truthfully, averting his gaze as he tried to edge past her, and winced at the sight of the figure displayed on the till. "Oh, blimey, what the heck…?"

"Don't say I've been naughty," she said coyly, tossing her hair over her shoulder in her best imitation of her favourite screen idol.

"I don't believe it…." He was saved from saying what he really thought by the bell tinging at the entrance. The tousled head of Jim Berry, the accountant appeared and he burst breezily into the shop.

"Cashed up already - that's the stuff. Can I bank the takings then?" He took one look at Albert's red face and clenched fingers, and continued quickly, "Ah, the inimitable Mrs Foxey. Evening, Mavis. Till still working, is it?" He glanced at the total and whistled, getting out his calculator. "My word, been buying up the shop again, have we?"

Mavis pulled herself up. "I consider that remark most uncalled for, Mr Berry. I think I'll go home where I'm wanted."

"Well, that's something – old man working late again, is he?"

"Oooh! That does it! I'm not staying here a minute longer." Catching sight of a tramp lurking outside and recognising Bimbo, the local walking talking Post Office, she added loudly, "…and you can tell your Albert Bridge to keep his hands to himself in future. Goodbye, and don't expect me back." Sweeping her things together Mavis sailed past them, satisfied she had done her bit to get the rumour started.

"Wait a minute, Mavis," Albert called after her hastily as he juggled with the keyboard. "I'm sure he didn't mean it, did you, Jim?"

Slam.

Albert sighed. "That's torn it. What did you want to go and say a thing like that for, you idiot." He ran a hand through his hair in exasperation. "What was she going on about, anyway?"

"Sorry, Bert," Jim apologised with a grin. "Couldn't resist that – I bet I know where she's off to…"

But Albert could only think of his own problems. "That's another volunteer gone – you know how difficult it is to replace them, especially in the holidays. Now what am I going to do?"

Jim heaved a sigh. "Never mind, I'll cover her shift for a while, until you find someone."

Albert relented. "That's all right – you do too much as it is." He looked at the figures and sighed. "I suppose we'd better get the takings agreed, otherwise I'll be in the doghouse at the bank – that's the third time this week."

"Right," agreed his friend briskly. "Tell you what - you count the notes and I'll do the small change. We'll soon get it sorted."

Ten minutes later they both sat back satisfied, their immediate problem solved.

"That seems all right, Bert," said Jim, gathering the notes together. "Got a bag for this lot – not exactly a fortune, is it?"

"You can say that again," agreed Albert, feeling depressed at the thought, then dismissed it, determined to keep such nagging fears to himself.

As they reached for their coats, Jim said thoughtfully,

"Sorry about that, I forgot it was holiday time. What'll you do about…?" He left the question hanging in the air.

"We'll see. Leave it with me…" Albert turned the problem over in his mind as he switched on the alarm and locked the shop door behind them.

Emerging into the High Street, he took a deep breath of contentment he always felt at the familiar sight of the century old cottages wending their way down the cobbled street in front of them, blending beyond into a shimmering thin ribbon of sea on the distant horizon. Overlooking it all was the reassuring presence of his cottage a few yards away, and next door to that Hettie's and her smallholding, her pride and joy.

Waving a hand, he said thoughtfully, "Makes it all worthwhile somehow. It's a beautiful spot, isn't it?"

Jim nodded his agreement. "None better."

Stopping at Jim's car, Albert reminisced. "It's what first caught my eye when I came down here on that coach trip nearly five years ago, looking for somewhere to settle down before I retired – I've never regretted it, not once. Which reminds me, the shop's anniversary comes up soon," adding gloomily, "not that I'll be able to splash out on anything, the way things are going."

As he climbed in, Jim suggested a solution that might tide them over. "What you want is someone to help out until you can get straight. Which reminds me, that nice young Sally who teaches up at the school is always asking if there's something useful she can do in the holidays." In answer to Albert's blank look, he shook his head regretfully, "Though I doubt if that old battleaxe of a mother of hers would allow it – you know what Lady Courtney is like. I know," he added, struck by a sudden thought, "isn't that nephew of yours at a loose end? Perhaps he could give you a hand."

"Young William?" Albert pondered. "Might be worth trying – I don't think he's made up his mind yet about what he's going to do with himself. Got some idea at one time about becoming a painter, so I'm told..."

Jim laughed. "Tell him he can have a go at our old house whenever he wants. It needs a lick of paint."

"No, he's after a full blown career as an artist – although not all that long ago he was talking about doing some writing of sorts. Mind you, I don't know how he's going to manage on what little my brother was able to leave him after that accident," sighed Albert ruefully. "Aunt Ethel got the house and the job of keeping an eye on him, and I don't think she's pleased the way things are going." He rubbed his chin. "Come to think of it, that's not a bad idea. A spell in the shop might help him sort his ideas out. It might get him out of doing relief work on that local rag – can't see that leading anywhere. I'll see what Hettie thinks and let you know," he said, waving a hand in farewell before turning in at his front gate.

"At least, you don't have to come far to get the shop open," laughed Jim, as he adjusted his seatbelt. "See you…"

"Bye, Jim, and thanks for your help…"

He was still turning the problem over in his mind as he shut the gate behind him and turned to walk up the path to the front door.

"Hi there!"

Jerked out of his reverie, he looked up to see Hettie leaning out of an upstairs bathroom window next door, a cloud of steam billowing out around her.

"Give me a minute to throw something on and I'll come and let you in. I've got your favourite all ready for you."

"Cor!"

Conscious of hot breath fanning his neck, Albert turned, caught sight of Bimbo behind him gazing up at the sight, his mouth open. Having witnessed the hasty departure of Mavis leaving the shop in an agitated state a few minutes earlier, the tramp put two and two together with a sharp intake of breath.

"Cor!" he repeated, and without asking for his usual handout – knowing that eager faces would be only too willing to reward him after hearing his latest gossip - he hastily flung a leg over his bike and wobbled off down the High Street in search of the nearest pub and his first free drink of the day, ready to spread the word that promised to be one of the most rewarding scandals the village had ever known.

Cheered up by the thought of supper Albert dismissed Bimbo's ramblings, and finding there was still no news about his assistant waiting for him, made his way next door.

After giving him her usual welcome kiss, Hettie noticed something was amiss and tried to cheer him up.

"What's the matter, Bert?" she asked, easing off his jacket. "Don't worry about the post - I picked up some of yours when I was in earlier," she explained, as she noticed his eyes stray in that direction. "Come and sit down."

"Oh, blimey, that's all I need," he groaned after skimming through the letters and picking out the first one he recognised by the writing.

"What's up? Someone made an offer for the shop? Only joking. Bad news, is it?"

"Only that Jackie's had orders from the doc to take some more time off, that's all."

"Jackie – you don't mean your assistant?" Seeing his gloomy expression she added hastily, "Sit down and make yourself comfortable while I get you a cuppa."

In no time she was back with an encouraging beam and a steaming mug. "There you are, luv, I've tickled it up with some of your favourite tipple. Now tell me all about it."

After taking a sip, he smacked his lips appreciatively and feeling more relaxed told her about Mavis and the trouble with the till, before getting down to tucking into a welcome steak and kidney pie she placed before him.

"Thank goodness you're shot of her," was her verdict. "Silly old cow." Then she chuckled, "Jim's got her taped though, hasn't he? We all know about her afternoons with the lodger."

"Doesn't make it any better in the shop though, does it? I can do with all the help I can get just now. I don't know how much longer I can carry on the rate things are going."

"If only you'd let me help, Bert," she fussed. "You know we all want you to succeed."

"I know." He looked away, distracted by the sight of her look of eager devotion, and hurriedly swallowed the last mouthful. "That was delicious. Which reminds me, I must try to get hold of William tomorrow and see if I can get him to give a hand in the shop. It might help him decide what he wants to do with his life."

Hettie said without thinking, "If only I didn't have the animals to look after, I could come and help you more…"

Bert stopped her firmly and thrust the tempting idea from his mind, aware of his insecure financial position. "Don't worry – I'll manage somehow. I've still got my redundancy money and pension, such as it is."

"I know it was always something you wanted to do, but," she went on impulsively without thinking, "was it such a good idea to give up a such a safe job in insurance…" Seeing his reaction, she broke off and went on hurriedly, "to start something so different - when we're not getting any younger," she added tactfully.

He slapped the table in frustration. "That's just it. You don't understand, Het, I couldn't stand it any longer. I was getting so bored and frustrated!" Having got that off his chest, he brooded, "The thought of wasting the rest of my life dealing with other people's insurance until I retired was driving me dotty – I tell you, I even ended up checking my own life expectancy table. I woke up one morning and realised I had to do something different – anything was better than the life I was leading. So I decided to get away from it all and start up my own business - to be my own boss. It seemed to make sense and I still think I did the right thing. You've no idea what it means to be part of the village life, watching my own business grow as part of the community, instead of sitting at a desk and spending the rest of my working life in an office. Grr." He looked up, surprised at his own eloquence. "Sorry about that – I got carried away a bit."

"I'm sure you did the right thing – it's what you wanted," Hettie reassured him. Thinking back, she mused, "It's funny the way things have turned out - you've got the shop and I've got my animals. D'you think you've taken on too much though? Don't forget there's young William to think about."

Albert sighed. "Yes, and he doesn't seem to know what he wants."

"You'll be telling me you don't know what you want next," she tried hopefully, touching his hand.

Sensing he was on dangerous ground he pushed his chair back hurriedly. "I think it's time I got back. I've got all that paperwork to catch up on. Thanks for the supper – you spoil me."

"I never get the chance properly, do I?" She heaved a sigh, doing her best to look on the bright side. "Don't worry, things are bound to get better. I know," searching in her mind for a helpful way out, "what happened to that other brother of yours – Neil, isn't it? Couldn't he take some time off to help? Wasn't he some sort of high flyer in the civil service?"

"Not exactly," said Albert sheepishly, wondering how to put it as he always did when talking about his brother Neil, who ever since he could remember had always been frowned on by the other members of his family. "He… er… found it wasn't quite his cup of tea – too dull. He decided, like me, to go in for something more enterprising in the private sector. Something he could get his teeth into."

As he spoke, he thought back to the last time he saw his young brother. Neil hadn't actually bitten anyone. But he certainly left one of the bobbies sucking his hand that time, and it had taken half a dozen reinforcements to persuade him to accompany them down to the station, while still protesting his innocence, after leading a revolt by fellow stallholders in one of his never-ending battles with some of the more officious members of the local Council.

Albert tried to imagine what a difference it would have made to have his go-getting young brother around before dismissing the idea regretfully. Neil had gone a bit too far this time to be in a position to do anything - he was still finishing off a community service sentence and wouldn't be around to help anyone for a while. Albert was an upright law-abiding creature, and although he loved his brother dearly, the thought of what Neil might do to improve the present situation made him quake inwardly.

He continued hastily, "No, I think he's a bit tied up at the moment – I'll try young William instead and see how he's fixed."

As she waved him off she called out encouragingly, "Don't worry. We're right behind you, Bert – and don't forget William, I'm sure he won't mind you asking."

"Don't worry, I will," called back Albert, relieved at the change of conversation. "I don't think they work him too hard on that local rag of his – I expect he'll be glad of the chance to help." To himself, he added, "Heaven help me if he doesn't…"

Chapter Two
A Proper Job

Albert had no need to worry on that score. Next morning, the sun was high in the sky before it got round to peeping through his nephew's bedroom window, revealing William still fast asleep in the middle of a bad dream, reliving the trauma of being sacked from the editorial office of the Snuggleton Globe newspaper. In his dream, he was sitting trapped at his desk, mesmerised by the incandescent face of Jock, the fiery sub-editor, glaring at him only inches away. A few minutes earlier, he dimly remembered, that same Scottish worthy had been complimenting him grudgingly on his report about the outcome of the local flower show competition that afternoon.

Unfortunately, at that moment a file happened to fall open on his desk, and a sample of his more imaginative artistic efforts slid out. As he handed them back Jock gave a passing indifferent glance at some of the figures the drawings revealed, mostly quick impressions of the villagers taking part, William had dashed off while waiting for the competition results to be announced. At first, his lips twitched in dour appreciation at the sight of one of the more notorious local characters who appeared to be tied to a rocket, with a label affixed, inviting onlookers to light the match. His faint smile vanished and his face began to assume a purple tinge as he took in a group of Council notables, headed by the Mayor about to present the prizes, flanked by the Town Clerk and another person who looked increasingly familiar.

If William had been content with mere lifelike impressions, all would have been well. But as the time passed waiting for the announcements he had grown increasingly bored and the figures began to turn into fantasy doodles, until the Mayor started to look more like an inebriated cow, the Town Clerk resembled a waddling duck, and the third provoked a furious reaction from the sub-editor, causing him to stiffen and point at it with a quivering finger, "And who…is that, may I ask?"

"Oh, that?" coughed William, trying to cover up the offending drawing casually.

The sub-editor snatched it away, and peered at it more closely. "Is that...thing...supposed to be me?"

William laughed nervously. "Why, what makes you think that?"

"Why?" snorted the sub angrily. "Look at it, you... you..." Speech almost failed him before he could get the words out. "Because... he's wearing a kilt with 'Jock' plastered all over it," he spluttered, "that's why." His voice swelled dangerously, "And he's holding a bottle of whisky, and he's...got his arms around the Town Clerk!"

Aware suddenly of some sniggers in the background from the other reporters trying hard not to listen, the sub-editor vented his fury on the hapless William. "Is this what I pay you for, producing r-rubbish like this?"

"Well, no, not all the time," admitted William, trying to be fair. "Only when there's nothing else to do."

"Well, you're wrong there, laddie, there is ... and you're *fired.*" In his fury he snatched up a ruler and beat a tattoo on the desk to add emphasis to his remarks. The noise went on and on, reverberating in William's mind until he finally came to in bed with a splitting headache, and the sound of someone banging on his bedroom door.

"Are you in there, nephew? Open this door at once!"

With a great effort, William forced himself to climb gingerly out of bed, and as soon as the room steadied around him, made a wavering lunge for the door. Scrabbling for the handle, he found it wouldn't open and looking down discovered why. The key was in the lock – he must have turned it last night to stop his aunt seeing the state he was in.

"The door must have stuck," he called out feebly, and pulling it open nearly fell over in the process. Focusing his eyes with an effort, he at first made out two images glaring at him accusingly, before they merged into the formidable figure of his Aunt Ethel.

Seeing his condition, she sniffed suspiciously. "And what time did you get home last night, pray?"

William waved a hand vaguely as he tried to concentrate and sift through his elusive memory. "Can't remember exactly… not too late. The lads were celebrating – couldn't refuse, could I?" he added hastily, anticipating the next question.

"That's as may be," she said grimly. "I only ask because the milkman went past on his early morning round soon afterwards. And what were you celebrating at that unearthly time, I would like to know?"

William had a mental vision of a ring of grinning faces, as the other reporters from the office reached out and lifted him shoulder high before marching into the pub to celebrate.

"Ah… I believe they were saying goodbye to someone leaving the paper."

"He must have been very popular, is all I can say." She sniffed again.

Her words conjured up a vision of his old pal, Malcolm, just returned from a back-packing trip to Sydney, wiping his eyes as he chortled over the details of William's parting remarks to the sub-editor. "Mate, we've all been dying to say something like that for months, but never had the courage. Good on you." And followed it up by thrusting yet another pint of ale in his hands.

Shaking off the memory of the seemingly un-ending row of empty glasses, William groped for a suitable answer and ended up scratching his head, "I don't know about that." Then deciding to nerve himself up to it, he took a deep breath and began bravely. "Now, I know you've never been very keen on me working on that local paper, Auntie…"

"Waste of time – what you need is a proper job," she broke in sharply.

Encouraged, William continued, "so I've decided to give it up."

"About time too," was her verdict. "I'm glad you're seeing sense at last, because your Uncle Albert phoned. He wants to see you, so look slippy." She eyed him up and down. "While you're at it, you can get me a paper. Here you are – mind you bring back the change. And take that silly grin off your face, you look a mess," was her parting shot.

Later, after working up the courage to take a cold shower followed by a brisk rub down, William began to feel faint signs of life stealing back into his limbs. Gulping down a quick mouthful of scalding coffee and coughing over it, he held his head to stop the throbbing and made for the front door.

Watching his unsteady progress up the High Street, Aunt Ethel shook her head. "Well, it's up to you, Albert. Heaven help the pair of you, is all I can say."

Labouring up the cobbled street, William concentrated on following a straight line, taking deep breaths every now and then to help him carry on. At last, standing in front of his Uncle's shop he took an extra deep breath and pushing the door open, looked in. His first impulse was to check the latest edition of the Snuggleton Globe tucked away on the bottom shelf, half expecting to see accusing headlines about himself. Reassured, he dropped it back hastily and glanced around.

"Hi, anybody about?"

A head bobbed up behind the centre stand revealing the anxious face of his Uncle Albert. Seeing William, he looked relieved. "Oh, it's you, William. Just the man, I've been trying to get in touch with you. Are you doing anything just now?"

"No," admitted William guardedly. "Why, what's up?"

"Not working on that local rag today?"

William debated, wondering how to put it. "Well, not exactly."

"Good. You can help us out on the counter then." Seeing William hesitate, he added hastily. "It's only until Hettie can take over."

Mistaking William's slow witted response for reluctance, he urged, "I wouldn't ask if we weren't so short handed. Can you do it, or can't you?"

"Of course," agreed William half-heartedly, trying to clear his head. "Anything to help out. What do you want me to do?"

Albert put down his order pad hurriedly. "Right, come over here, and I'll give you a quick rundown on the till – I'm expecting a delivery, so I can't spend too long." Standing William in front of the till, he explained which keys to press and how it worked in quick staccato fashion, ending with, "got that? Good, then I'll leave you to it." He patted him on the back, "I know it's all new to you, lad, but do the best you can. Shout if there's anything you don't understand."

William eyed the keyboard doubtfully. "She won't be too long, will she?"

He was still grappling with the information his uncle had flung at him, and holding his head whilst trying to concentrate on what he was supposed to do, when the shop door opened with a click and in strolled one of the most beautiful girls William had ever seen. In an instant, he realised this was the defining moment of his life. Compared with her all the other girls he had known disappeared in a puff of smoke - this was the real thing. With her blue eyes, blonde hair and trim figure, she ticked all the boxes as a tailor-made answer to his dreams. It was uncanny – he was so overcome, he just stood there drinking her in.

Thinking him a little shy, Sally gave him a friendly smile. "Hello," she said brightly. "You're new, aren't you?" As he tried to stutter a reply, she turned and called out gaily to Albert to cover an awkward pause, "What's all this I hear about you wanting some help, Mr Bridge? Anything I can do?"

Albert dropped his order form again, and hurried forward. "Why, it's Miss Sally – how nice to see you. Did I hear right – you want to help? Are you sure you can spare the time, what with all your teaching up at the school?"

Sally laughed, "I'm sure they won't miss me if I do a stint now and then on my day off. But I see you already have some help, won't I be in the way?"

William stood there entranced, then realising she was looking at him questioningly, came to with a start. "No, no, of course not," he blurted out eagerly, "would she, Uncle?"

Albert beamed. "You just come along whenever you want m'dear. I'll get Hettie to show you how it all works – she's busy just now, helping out with the pigs. William's just started, otherwise I'm sure he'd be pleased to show you the ropes."

"I'd be happy to show you what I know," offered William quickly, at last finding his voice. "If you'll come around the back, I'll run through it with you."

"Good, that shouldn't take long," laughed his uncle, relieved at his nephew's change of heart and amused at his sudden interest. "I'll carry on with the orders then. Het won't be long now."

"Well, perhaps it would be better to wait for Hettie," Sally temporised, then catching sight of a face peering through the window, she dived behind the counter. "Quick, it's Clive, I don't want him to see me."

She had barely stopped talking when the shop door opened and a young man looked in, a supercilious expression on his face. Seeing William, he drawled, "I say, has Miss Frobisher-Courtney been in lately?"

"Who?" enquired William blankly. "Sorry, don't know the name," he added truthfully.

"Never mind," the young man said curtly and the door closed again.

As soon as his head passed the window, William bent down, "Okay, I think he's gone."

As Sally began to get up William saw the head coming back past the window again, accompanied by a familiar face.

"Wait," he whispered urgently. "He's got Hettie with him."

The door opened and Hettie's voice boomed out as she pulled the protesting figure in behind her, followed by her pigman accompanied by a strong farmyard smell. "Sally, are you there? I've got a young man asking after you."

As soon as she released him Clive jerked his arm free and backed away hurriedly, holding a handkerchief to his nose. "Some other time, Madam," he gabbled. "I've just remembered an urgent appointment – must dash," and with a last wild look around he turned and bolted.

Hettie looked around in surprise. "What's the matter with him? Oh, there you are, what are you doing down there?" as Sally rose behind the counter, trying not to giggle.

"I don't think he's used to the fresh country air," said William tactfully.

Albert's head bobbed up. "Is that you, Het? Blimey, open the door, someone, you'll frighten all our customers away."

"If you can't stand a bit of honest country air," began Hettie indignantly.

Seizing the excuse William motioned Sally towards the door. "It's almost lunchtime, Uncle. We'll just go and grab a bite – see you later."

"Before you go, lad, you might get Hettie to give the till the once-over to make sure it's ship-shape. I'm up to my eyes in it right now."

"Of course." Hettie bustled forward. "Make way, young William, while I check it's all bumps-a-daisy."

"Sure," said William hurriedly, backing away from the aroma, "it's all yours."

"Now let's see," beamed Hettie, pulling out a roll of receipts. "Ooh, haven't you been a naughty boy. I see you haven't cancelled out the mistakes you've made. Don't worry, I'll soon fix it."

Her hands darted over the keyboard like a concert pianist, and she giggled as she did so.

"I call these naughties – just like your uncle sometimes." She glanced at Albert hopefully.

Pretending not to hear, Albert butted in hastily and waved them off. "I think you'd better go before the rush starts. Off you go, both of you – oh, and you might drop this packet off at old Mrs Sturgis on the way." He sniffed. "And while you're at it leave the door open, for heaven's sake."

Outside, William apologised. "Sorry about that – Uncle's a bit short handed at the moment. I hope you don't mind if we make that delivery on the way. It's probably another of his old pensioners who can't make it to the shop."

"Ah, well, I suppose every little helps."

"Knowing Uncle, I doubt if he ever charges her – I sometimes wonder how he ever makes any profit," apologised William.

"Then it's a good thing he's got Hettie to help him," offered Sally. She heaved a sigh of relief. "He certainly got that awful Clive off my back."

Over a salad lunch at Ma's Snackbar across the road they relaxed, and William seized on her remark about Clive as an excuse to find out more about her.

"Who was that chap, Clive – is he making a nuisance of himself?"

Sally grimaced. "Oh, he's another of those pests Mummy is always trying to pass off on me. She wants me to get to know all the 'right people', as she puts it - she's always doing it." Seeing his mystified look, she sighed. "I suppose I should be used to it by now. Just because Dad got landed with the family title and all that rot, she thinks nothing is too good for me – she's a terrible snob, I'm afraid."

William nearly speared himself with a succulent morsel at the news and looked worried. "Does that mean you've got some sort of title as well?"

"No, thank goodness," she grinned faintly. "It's my big brother, Lance, who's heir to the title, thank heavens. Don't look so worried," she added, noticing his expression. "I'm still 'Sally', to all my friends."

"But," he picked his words carefully, "what does your mother think of you working part-time in the shop?"

"She'd have been delighted I expect, if she'd been alive." For a moment, Sally's eye took on a wistful look.

"Oh, I'm sorry."

"That's all right. She died soon after I was born, so I never did get to know what she would have liked." She shook herself out of a daydream. "No, it's my stepmother who's the wicked witch. She doesn't know, and I don't intend to tell her – I expect she'll hit the roof when she does hear," she mused thoughtfully.

"Then why?"

"Well, as a matter of fact, I felt sorry for your Uncle Albert– after what happened with that awful Foxey woman." Seeing the puzzled look on his face, she laughed. "I'm not explaining this very well, am I?"

"Foxey woman?" William repeated groping. "Who's she?"

"You mean to say you haven't heard? Apparently she tried to make a pass at your uncle in the shop yesterday to win a bet or something and it didn't come off, so she's going around accusing him of all sorts of things and trying to stir up trouble."

"Wow," said William, doing his best to digest the news. "I'd better let him know. If Hettie hears about it, she'll be up in arms."

"A tough lady, is she?"

William nodded. "And how. Mind you, Uncle Albert can look after himself – it must have taken quite a bit of courage to take early retirement and set up this village shop idea of his. It's something he's always wanted to do."

"And are you planning to take after him?" Sally couldn't help being curious.

William looked uncomfortable. "Well, I said I'd help him out for the time being."

Then getting it off his chest, he blurted out, "I really want to do something different, on my own." Reassured by her look of sympathy, he confided, "Like a painter or, better still, a writer, but I haven't had much luck so far."

Trying to be helpful, Sally suggested, "Perhaps you ought to start off by getting experience on a newspaper or a magazine, or something like that."

"As a matter of a fact," William hesitated, "I have been doing some part-time work on the local rag."

"That's a good start then," encouraged Sally. "How are you getting on?"

"Not too well, I must admit," confessed William, shifting uncomfortably in his seat. He paused for a moment, looking at her to see how she would take it, then reassured by her expression it all came out with a rush.

Halfway through his tale Sally started to giggle, and when he came to the bit where the sub-editor voiced his outrage about the cartoon-like impressions she collapsed, wiping her eyes.

"Don't," she said weakly. "I can just imagine it. Why, do you realise - you've got enough there to start a book off already."

"Well," he shuffled his feet, "I've knocked out one or two chapters based on some of my previous jobs, but I haven't been able to interest anyone in it yet."

"What sort of things?" she wanted to know. "It couldn't get much funnier than that."

He pondered. "I've done all sorts of odd things, I suppose. There was the time I helped out on a fairground," he brooded, "and I had to escort the local beauty queen and take her up in a swing for a publicity photo. It wasn't my fault the blessed swing broke down and we got dumped in the swimming pool next door, and she came out with hardly a stitch on. Then there was time I was doing work experience on an animal farm when a wretched iguana charged at me in the feeding pen and I only had a few seconds to jump up on the counter, and he nearly got the manager instead. Oh and the time we had a goat and I built a hut for it, and the wretched animal climbed up the wall inside and made it collapse."

"Oh, don't," cried Sally, overcome. "Have you got anything finished I can look at? I'd love to see it."

"Would you really?" William brightened. "I think I could dig it out, if you really mean it."

"Oh, yes," said Sally definitely. "Tell me, how did you get started on all this – what did your dad think of it all?"

William went silent for a moment and cleared his throat. "Dad wanted me to follow him into the engineering business, and Mum wanted me to be," he suddenly looked bashful, "a ballet dancer. But it didn't work out."

For a moment Sally tried to conjure up in her mind the idea of William dressed up in a tutu, but gave up. Then she followed up his line of thought, her curiosity aroused. "Why was that?"

"They both got killed in a car crash," he said simply, "and Aunt Ethel was landed with the job of looking after me."

Sally touched his arm impulsively. "I'm sorry - I didn't know." The sudden contact made William jump self-consciously and left Sally uneasy in her mind at the unexpected feeling he had aroused.

They were both quiet for a moment, then William went on thoughtfully, "Mum was the artistic one, you see, I suppose that's where I get this urge to express myself. Silly, isn't it?"

Shaking herself, Sally was quite firm. "No, of course not, it's quite natural. I always wanted to be a racing driver – believe it or not. Dad was thrilled at the idea, but I never heard the last of it from Ma – you'd have thought I wanted to rob a bank or something. That's why I decided to take up teaching – at least it got me out of the house."

"What did your stepmother think of that?"

"She thought I'd soon get sick of it. Funny, I suppose," she grimaced, "when you think about it. She's always been standing up for women's rights, and all that. I suppose it's different when it happens in your own family."

William tried to conjure up a mental picture of the situation but failed. "Mmm."

"Anyway," Sally got back to her original intention. "You dig out those stories and let me have a look – I just might be able to find someone to cast a professional eye on them."

She thought reluctantly of Clive for a moment, remembering vaguely he was supposed to be in advertising or something, perhaps he would know, and went on quickly, "One of those men that mother's always foisting on me might be able to help, you never know."

"But why are you offering to do all this?" William was mystified. "You must get this from your six formers all the time, when they're leaving and looking for jobs."

Sally gave a light laugh, not too sure herself. "We shop workers must stick together, remember. Just leave that side of it to me," trying to convince herself she was acting more like an understanding sister. "See you later after school," she promised hopefully, "about teatime."

Chapter Three
Word Gets Around

Sally didn't have long to put her theory into practice. Soon after leaving William she was nearly run over by a sports car that came hurtling around the corner and braked suddenly in front of her.

Getting to her feet shakily, she came face to face with Clive, the driver.

"Can't you look where you're going?" he accused in a blind panic, his eyes fixed anxiously on his car. "It was all your fault," he added automatically, bending down to wipe a speck of dust off the bumper. "You could have caused a serious accident. I don't know what the owner will say." Then realising who it was he was taken aback. "Oh, sorry, Sally, didn't see it was you."

Trembling, she managed, "I see, that makes all the difference, does it?" Then remembering she was about to ask a favour, she modified her tone. "Oh, I'm all right, just a few scratches, I think. Forget it."

"I'm dreadfully sorry," Clive apologised with a weak smile. "I was just on my way to have a spot of tea with your mother, Lady Courtney. I didn't want to be late."

"Stepmother," corrected Sally automatically. "Don't let me keep you then."

"You sure you're all right – there's nothing I can do?" he asked, half looking at his watch. "Can I give you a lift anywhere?"

"Wait, there is as it happens." She attempted a smile as she pulled herself together. "I don't suppose by any chance you know any publishers or agents, in your line of business?"

Clive shoved his business card back in his pocket, realising that the description 'car dealer – we buy and sell anything' didn't quite live up to the line of business she had in mind. "Well," he said quickly, trying to look modest, "as a matter of a fact, being in PR I do have quite a bit of pull with one or two of the top boys– they often ring me up when they're after a bargain."

"Good," beamed Sally, settling herself in the passenger seat. "In that case you can drop me at the school, and I'll tell you about it on the way."

"So you see," she wound up as they came in sight of the school, "it would mean an awful lot to William if you could help him in any way. It would give him confidence and put him on the right path as well as helping his uncle make the shop a success. Especially," she started to say, "after all those rumours about that wretched Foxey woman," then stopped quickly, realising she had said too much.

Stifling his alarm at her enthusiasm about a possible rival, and making a mental note to find out more about the Foxey character she mentioned, he assured her craftily, "Of course, I'll do all I can to help. I can't promise anything but leave it to me. Let me have a copy of whatever he's done and meanwhile I'll find out who's the best man to contact. And I think this is where I drop you off."

And as he braked, a pile of papers shot out of his glove box and landed on her lap.

Picking them up and noting the name on the log book before replacing it, she repeated the name wonderingly, "Ron Smith? Who's that when he's at home?"

Laughing it off nervously, Clive stuffed the papers back and lied, "Oh, nothing to worry about - one of the previous owners, you know." Cursing to himself that he hadn't got rid of the forged papers when they'd cleaned the car out he joked unconvincingly, "You get masses of paperwork when you take on a car, believe me, and talking about paperwork don't forget to get me a copy of that young man's efforts, so I can get someone to see it." *And a fat lot of good it will do him if I have anything to do with it*, he promised himself.

As it happened, he had to satisfy his hostess with some of her own searching questions before he was able to put his ideas into practice.

Giving his encounter with Sally as an excuse for being late, he was rewarded with a sniff of displeasure. "Oh, how is the gel?" she enquired frostily, and without waiting for a reply she indicated a vacant seat on the terrace. "Sit there Clive do, while I get the maid to bring some tea and things." She rang a bell, and to bridge the conversation, she moved into her customary line of enquiry to satisfy herself as to his position in society. "Do say, if you don't find it comfortable."

"No, it's absolutely splendid, Lady Courtney," he assured her hastily.

"It's actually Lady Frobisher Courtney, you know," she pointed out regally. "My husband is most insistent people get it right, otherwise these old fashioned family courtesies just get lost for posterity - I expect you find the same thing."

He was about to reply when the maid plonked the tray down on the table and nearly spilt the milk.

"Careful, Mary, not there, mind what you're doing," she warned with a hint of steel in her voice.

"Now then," as she passed a cup across to Clive, "do tell me how your family is getting on. You're one of the Suffolk Brands - a junior branch, I believe," she added condescendingly. "Let me see, I suppose it goes back a few years or so?"

Clive rescued his cup as it slid off his saucer in his eagerness to agree with her. "Oh, yes, many hundreds of years." Then, aware there might be a conflict of interests, he added hastily, "Not as far back as your own line extends, I am sure."

Her placid smile of contentment confirmed he had said the right thing and he sat back with a sigh of relief. The next half hour was spent by his hostess probing his background, with Clive crossing his fingers and making himself sound like a cross between a financial wizard and an up and coming leader of society. Even Clive found himself being impressed by his replies, which was not unnatural for a conman of his ability.

"And from what you were saying, I gather your business prospects are quite well established."

"Of course, we are still expanding," he assured her, hurriedly dismissing a picture of a ramshackle garage from his mind. "We're no Rockefeller, but I am sure he would be happy to learn a thing or two from us in the way we do business. I'm not in a position to mention any names, you understand, but yesterday I had a tempting offer to take us over - from a leading finance company."

He omitted to mention it was in connection with a notice of foreclosure on his garage for not keeping up his payments, but his reply brought out a satisfied smile of acceptance.

He was beginning to feel he had passed the test, when she homed in on the reason for his invitation. "Of course," she pointed out airily, "our little estate is not vast – I forget how far it extends offhand, some three or four thousand acres or so I believe, but it will mean a lot of responsibility for someone to look after one of these days, and my husband and I will not be here to keep an eye on things forever."

She fixed him with a benevolent smile. "I don't mind telling you this in confidence, Clive, as I know it will go no further, but I am most disappointed in Lancelot, our eldest boy. He's shown absolutely no interest in taking on the responsibilities of the estate. And as for Sally," she sighed. "First of all it was motor racing, now her latest fad is teaching. If only you knew how she upsets me." She pulled herself together and squared up like a sergeant major. "It needs someone with a wider vision. Now, if only Sally had found the right man to guide her, to take all the right decisions on her behalf," she paused and looked at him invitingly. "If only I knew there was someone to take on the challenge, someone I could trust."

"You need have no fears on that score, as far as I am concerned," Clive assured her eagerly. "You must know how much I care for Sally and," he almost added 'the estate' as his mind dwelled lovingly on the money it would bring in, then quickly amended it to, "all the responsibilities such a position would entail."

At his words, Lady Frobisher Courtney unbent in her regal attitude to bestow a signal mark of blessing. "Dear Clive, you may kiss me. And now, if you'll excuse me I, have to meet an old friend of the family, Ed Newman, who is over here from the States to set up an English branch of his security business. He's such a dear friend." *And one*, she added grimly to herself, *who will, I hope, help that useless son of mine get a job and wake his ideas up.*

As he bent to do her bidding and kiss her on the cheek, Clive took the opportunity to spike William's guns.

"I will do my best to make her happy, you can be sure of that." He felt his way, "I hate to be the one to spoil such a happy occasion, but you perhaps don't know that Sally is being distracted in other directions at the moment."

"Well, I know she's taken up with this ridiculous idea of teaching, but I hope you will help to put a stop to that!" she retorted frostily.

"If that was the only problem," he added, with just the right note of simulated anxiety.

"What else is there?" she barked, rising to the bait.

"Far be it for me to break any family confidences," he began, taking a swift look to see her reaction. "But I gather she's taking more than just a friendly interest in a young man at the village store."

"What? The village store? You don't mean *our* village store?" Lady Courtney sat up with a jerk, giving the impression that someone had stuck a large hat pin in her amply padded rear. "Who is that, may I ask?"

Gratified at her response, Clive went on smoothly. "His name is William, I am told. I understand he's been taken on by his uncle, Albert Bridge, the owner, while he's looking for a job. Unless the store folds up first, of course."

His host started making mewing noises. "A...tradesman..."

"Yes," Clive was enjoying himself. "According to reliable sources, the shop is on its last legs anyway - and you've heard the rumours going around about Albert?"

"No?" gasped his hostess faintly.

Clive leaned forward with relish. "Well, I hear there's some kind of scandal about Albert Bridge and one of his helpers at the shop, someone called Mavis Foxey, it seems."

"That's enough. I don't want to hear any more," wailed Lady Frobisher Courtney. "We must stop it before it gets any further. Oh the disgrace of it. Where's my husband? No, Henry's never here when I want him. I'll deal with this myself. Take me to the shop immediately, d'you hear!"

Meanwhile, back at the shop, William's mind was in ferment on a different matter.

"What time do you call this?" Albert greeted him as he dived behind the counter and found his uncle coping with a queue of customers. "I thought you'd forgotten us."

"Sorry," he mumbled, taking over, "got talking to Sally." Then remembering the gossip that Sally had passed on, he tried to warn his uncle. "That reminds me - I must tell you…"

"Not now, later," said Albert hurriedly, seeing the queue beginning to build up. "Be a good lad and find some more bags will you, we seem to have run out."

By the time William had hunted down a new supply the queue was getting longer and there was no chance to have a last minute word about Mavis.

However much he tried to keep his thoughts concentrated on the waiting customers, the exciting possibility that Sally might find someone interested in his story and get it published made it very difficult for him to work out what he was supposed to be doing amid the growing confusion around him. People kept bringing up their items of shopping and dumping them on the counter – anything from assorted bread rolls to giant cornets – and waiting patiently for him to enter them up on the till, but as each item was presented to him it was transformed in his mind's eye into a copy of his new book with his name in fiery letters across the front cover.

To complicate matters, some of the goods on display did not have a price tag on them for some reason, and William had to ask them to hang on for a minute while he dived off to ask. But oddly enough, the customers did not seem to be at all concerned about the cost. Judging by the inquisitive expression in their eyes they were nerving themselves to ask about something else, but didn't quite know how to put it – particularly as the subject in question was his Uncle Albert.

As William soon realised by the look on their faces, it was evident word had already got around, and there was only one topic of interest in the waiting queue.

People were nudging each other, and suddenly a shout went up as old Harry, one of the regulars, hobbled in leaning on his stick, wheezing as he tried to get the words out. "Hi, Bert, did yer manage... you know?"

He was shouldered aside by widow Wendy who shook her umbrella fiercely at Albert, "Repent while there is still time, oh miserable sinner."

"What the 'eck's she talking about?" whispered Albert, looking up blankly.

"I keep trying to tell you, Uncle," broke in William, trying to get his attention. "Sally said…"

"Never mind," urged Albert, taking note of the sudden influx of numbers. "Just keep on serving – blimey, this is good for business."

As each customer was served in turn, they ended up about to ask something then unable to get the words out, muttered 'thanks' and shuffled off with their purchases, some giggling and others asking after Albert and giving knowing looks. It wasn't until Ted the painter turned up that he put the question bluntly the others had been dying to ask.

"Two ounces of my usual baccy, son," he began, and directly he was served he came out with it. "Well, did he or didn't he?" he winked, as he rolled a cigarette, lit it and squinted through the haze.

"Pardon?" queried William, handing over the change distractedly.

"Old Albert," Ted repeated. "Did he pull it off with our Mavis?"

"No, it's not Mavis who's doing it," William corrected absently, his mind still on the book.

"It's Sally." Seeing Ted's mystified expression, he explained, "you know, Sally who teaches up at the school."

"You're kidding," said Ted glancing sideways at Albert, admiration mingled with wonder, his estimation of his old friend as a lady's man going up in leaps and bounds. "Well, I'm blessed, I never knew he had it in him."

William followed his gaze, and clapped his forehead. "Oh no, you misunderstand me. I was talking about my book – Sally's promised to look at it."

Hearing the tail end of his remark, someone behind gasped and uttered, "Coo, fancy that."

Diverted for a moment, Ted looked interested. "Oh, you're going to be a writer, are you? That reminds me, did I tell you about my poems?" He was about to elaborate when William interrupted him hastily, seeing the queue building up again.

"No, why don't you bring them in some other time." He leaned forward confidentially. "Ted, it's not true about Uncle, she's trying to stir up trouble." As the people behind craned to listen in, he made sure they could all hear. "She tried it on for a silly bet and it didn't come off."

Unfortunately, his words were taken literally and only served to make the matters worse.

"What didn't?" someone in the background wanted to know.

"Well, I never, that young missy up at the school." The message was passed back.

Eyes goggling, the woman in the blue blouse craning her head at the back hissed. "Wait till I see Ernie."

"Nothing did," repeated William, raising his voice in exasperation. "Ask Uncle, he'll tell you."

"Oh, yes," said Ted knowingly, "I believe you, young William. Mind you," he reflected, starting to roll another cigarette as he contemplated, "anyone trying it on with that Mavis would need to have his head examined to start with – isn't that right, Squire?" as Albert moved up to join them, attracted by the crowd gathering.

"What's that?" inquired Albert. "Who wants his head examined?"

Pulling him away from the counter, William gabbled desperately, "I was trying to tell you, Uncle – Mavis is stirring it up about, you know." He looked around to make sure nobody could hear, but his voice was almost drowned in the background gossip. "What happened in the shop yesterday, and now they're trying to make out that Sally's got something to do with it."

"Oh," enlightenment came to Albert as he surveyed the sea of faces. "Is that what it's about?" He slapped his hand down on the counter and burst out fiercely. "It's all a lot of codswallop, as well you know, Ted. Mavis is nothing but a tiresome old gossip trying to win a bet– she's got not nothing better to do with her time, and as for that nice young Miss Sally, well…"

"Someone talking about me?" came a cheerful voice, as the young lady in question breezed in the shop. Immediately, the customers parted to let her through, waiting in anticipation.

Even Ted looked embarrassed. "Morning all – time I was off."

"What's the matter with him?" Sally looked around for the answer. "Have I got the plague or something?"

William broke the uncomfortable silence. "I'm afraid it may have been something I said."

Coming to his rescue, Albert dismissed his remarks. "Nonsense. Just because that Mavis didn't win her bet, that's what started it all. Mind you," he meditated, "it hasn't done me any harm, come to think about it. We've had the best takings all week."

Sally laughed in sympathy. "That's what comes of being a hotbed of gossip – I heard all about it," she added impishly. "You're quite the village lothario."

Noticing the anguished look coming from William, she added lightly, "Well, where's this masterpiece of yours? Am I going to be permitted to see it then?"

Sheepishly, William fished under the counter and hauled out a battered bundle, tied up with ribbon. "It's in a bit of a mess, I'm afraid. You won't like it."

"How d'you know? Anyway, I've asked Clive to have a look at it," she grimaced. "Apparently he's a big noise in PR. He knows everyone, so he tells me."

"But I thought," William started to say.

Sally smiled brightly. "I know, but I couldn't find anyone else who might help. Besides,

Mummy's always telling me to make friends in the right quarter, so I might as well get him to do something useful. Must dash, I'll let you know, byee."

Aware of a sudden hush behind her, she turned and caught sight of a grim upright figure entering the shop, clearing an empty space right and left as the villagers scrambled to get out of her way.

"Oh, lor'," gasped Sally apprehensively. "It's Ma."

Surveying the scene haughtily through her lorgnette, Lady Frobisher Courtney barked, "What is the meaning of this sordid business you've got yourself into, young lady? I demand to know what it's all about."

Taken aback, Sally stalled, "Why, Ma what are you doing here?"

"Never mind what I'm doing - what are you up to, young lady, is more to the point. I think you'd better come home and explain it all to your father."

In desperation, Sally fired off a blind shot at random in an attempt to divert her.

"I thought you were supposed to be meeting your American friend, Mr Newman?"

Some of Lady Courtney's fire evaporated, and she started getting flustered. "Was it today he's coming? I thought it was tomorrow – that secretary of mine must have got it wrong again."

Sally asked innocently, "Did you say it was two o'clock? It's nearly that now."

"Oh my goodness, so it is. I'd forgotten. What with," she paused distractedly, "what is that ghastly noise out there - what is going on?"

But as she spoke, she became aware she was losing the attention of her audience. There was a confusing medley of raised noises outside, and those left in the queue were craning their necks and beginning to melt away, anxious not to miss anything that promised to sound like a fight. A scuffle seemed to be developing, and she was nearly knocked over in the rush to get out and witness it at first hand.

Whipping out her lorgnette, Lady Courtney turned. "If this is the kind of rabble you attract, I think it's about time I took my custom elsewhere," she began. Then taking a closer look, she added frigidly, "What a disgusting spectacle. It appears to be some kind of brawl – why, isn't that the Mavis Foxey person I hear they're all talking about? And who's that with her? It looks as though it might be your wife, Mr Bridge. How undignified!"

But Albert had already flung off his apron and pushing her aside was already halfway out of the shop, ready to give his support to Hettie who was locked in combat with Mavis.

He was just in time to pull them apart when Mavis looked around, making sure she had an audience. "Get your hands off me. After what happened in the shop, I'll see your name is mud, you'll see."

"You lying hound," cried Hettie indignantly, diving back into the fray. The next moment Mavis staggered back, nursing a black eye.

It was all too much for Lady Courtney. She took hold of her daughter purposefully as she noticed her edging away, trying to make her escape. "Come with me, Sally," she ordered, pushing her way through the excited onlookers. "I won't have you consorting with this kind of rabble."

"But Ma, they're my friends," protested Sally.

"Nonsense," objected her mother, tightening her grip. "I particularly want you to meet Mr Newman. He has a daughter who I want you to get to know. I promised Ed-ward I'd find the right kind of people for her to meet."

Keeping her head down and avoiding the mad scramble around them she charged disdainfully through the throng, looking straight ahead, and in doing so barged right into the back of a stout man backing out of a taxi, knocking him flying.

"Say, what the heck?" the man wheezed as he struggled to pick himself up. "What's going on here – some sort of revolution?"

Collecting herself, Lady Courtney apologised profusely. "I'm dreadfully sorry – why it's Ed-ward – Ed-ward Newman. Please forgive me, I'd no idea."

Raising his Stetson in acknowledgement, her friend straightened up in bewilderment. "Why gee, it's Margery. I thought you said it was a quiet place around here?"

"Oh, it is normally," Lady Courtney assured him. "Very peaceful." She glanced around hurriedly. "Why don't we all go back and you can tell me all about your plans over a cup of tea. I see you have a taxi."

"Well darn it, that is mighty nice of you, Margery, but see here, Veronica, my little girl, is organising somewhere to stay. I guess I oughta find out what she's managed to come up with."

"Oh," said Lady Courtney, sounding a trifle put out. "Splendid, meanwhile may I introduce my gel, Sally. Sally, say hello to Mr Newman."

Edward Newman clasped her hand enthusiastically. "Hello, Sally. Gee this is swell, I can see you and my daughter Veronica will get on just fine. Why, here she is. Veronica, my dear, I want you to meet…"

Disregarding the introductions, his daughter interrupted impatiently, "Oh, there you are, Paw. I've been looking for you all over. The van's loaded up waiting, come along, what a mob."

Wheedling, her father tried to soothe her. "Okay, Vee, just coming. First, say hello to my good friend, Lady Courtney and her daughter, Sally. I'm sure you're going to get on just fine."

Thawing slightly at the mention of a title Veronica allowed, "How do, Lady Courtney?"

"Charmed, I'm sure," beamed Lady Courtney. "And this is my gel, Sally. You two must get together – I'm sure you'll find a lot in common."

"Hello," greeted Sally politely.

The two girls glanced at each other warily – Sally feeling slightly upstaged by the sophisticated outfit Veronica was wearing, and Veronica in turn feeling jealous of the wholesome image Sally presented.

"Say, Paw." Veronica returned to her immediate problem, ignoring the proffered hand. "Let's get going, you know what these removal men are like."

"Ah, sure, if you say so, Vee. If you'll excuse us, Margery, I guess we'd better see what they're up to – we don't want to upset anyone before we've even moved in."

"Moved in?" faltered Lady Courtney. "You mean you're planning to live here in the village?"

"Why sure, anything wrong in that? Where is the place, Vee honey, I forget?"

Veronica consulted a piece of paper. "It says here, 'The Forge, High Street' Come on, let's go see."

"The Forge?" puzzled Sally, turning to her stepmother. "Isn't that the cottage next to Hettie and the smallholding?"

Veronica wrinkled her nose in disgust. "Yeah, that's something we need to take up with the agents, Paw. There's some sort of pig farm alongside. They didn't tell us about that."

"Pig farm?" paled Lady Courtney. "That's almost next door to the village shop," her voice trailed off aghast.

"That's great," said Newman enthusiastically, beaming around happily at the mixed reaction to his news. "Why we'll have all our stores available on tap. I call that real neighbourly."

Chapter Four
Big Business Moves In

William set the alarm that night to make sure he got up early next morning in case Sally turned up with news about his book.

In fact, he got there at half past seven expecting to find the shop empty, but to his surprise Hettie was already hard at work, hastily unpacking bundles of newspapers that had just arrived, and beginning to tick them off against the delivery notes.

"Oh, there you are," Hettie broke off with a sigh of relief. "Can you give me a hand, luv? Your Uncle Albert's still getting over yesterday's dust up."

"Of course," William agreed, taking his jacket off. "What's up – is he all right?"

Hettie sounded worried. "The daft man tried to help when I got involved in that fight with that wretched Mavis woman yesterday, and got himself crocked up."

"Crocked up," echoed William, alarmed. "Does that mean he won't be in?"

"We'll see," said Hettie distractedly. "The doctor's promised to look in later to see how he is."

"So you've stepped in to lend a hand," finished William, relieved. "Here, let me," he helped her to set out the newspapers. Noticing her harassed face, he asked, concerned, "You look as if you could do with a lie-in yourself."

"Up half the night with Ferdie - thank heavens it's Saturday," she answered briefly. "Here - catch." She passed a file over. "There's a list of our regulars inside. If you could take out the copies they've ordered and put them under the counter ready for when they come in, that would be great."

"Ferdie?" said William confused. "I didn't know you had anyone staying with you?"

Hettie pulled a face. "Ferdie's the cow. I was up half the night with her – she's picked up a bug of some sorts. The vet's coming in later."

"Oh," acknowledged William with a cheeky grin. "I thought it might be your boyfriend."

"Chance would be a fine thing." Hettie heaved a sigh. "There's only one man in my life - and he doesn't seem to know I exist."

"Oh, and who's that?" asked William intrigued, as he bent down under the counter to place the marked-up copies ready for collection.

Hettie was saved from answering by the shop bell tinging.

"At last I've found somewhere open in this one-eyed joint."

The door opened to reveal a bored looking Veronica, who glanced around and sauntered over to the newspaper shelf, rifling idly through the available editions in some disgust. "Say, haven't you got any decent noospapers around here?"

About to point out they were not open yet, Hettie changed her mind, sensing new business, and dropped what she was doing to come forward with a bright smile of recognition, only too anxious to help her beloved Albert. "Oh, hello, you're our new next door neighbour, aren't you? You must be Veronica. Is there anything in particular you would like?"

At the mention of 'next door neighbour', Veronica reacted like a red rag to a bull. With the light of battle in her eyes she rounded on Hettie. "So you're the one with the flaming animal that's driving us all mad?"

"The poor thing's sick," cried Hettie defensively. "I was up all night looking after her."

"So were we – sick to death of the flaming noise, and let me tell you sumpin'." Veronica was just getting into her stride, when William stuck his head up, wondering what all the fuss was about.

Catching sight of his rugged good looks Veronica halted, her interest noticeably awakened. Her voice softened and took on a new note. "And who are you, stranger?"

Quick to take advantage of the lessening tension, Hettie hastened to make the introductions. "This is William. His Uncle Albert runs our village store here, and William's helping him make it expand – he's full of ideas." Seeing his hesitation, Hettie hurried on, "William, this is Veronica, our new next door neighbour – come and say 'hello'." To William, she explained brightly, "Veronica's father is planning to open up a new branch of his security firm over here, isn't that right, Veronica?"

"Why, sure," agreed Veronica, unable to keep her eyes off William. "I like a man with ideas. See here, we must get together now we've been introduced."

"Of course." William eyed her politely, after urgent prompting from Hettie.

Following some more hand signalling by Hettie behind Veronica's back, he searched around in his mind for a suitable follow-up. "Did I hear you say you were looking for something – a newspaper, or some groceries perhaps?"

For an answer, Veronica draped herself across the counter and leaned forward invitingly. "Well, I guess it's what you can do for me. See here, we've just hit town and need to stock up."

Trying not to stare at the looming curves confronting him, William stuttered, "Is there anything in particular you wanted?"

"Well, let's see." She shifted herself even closer. "I guess I'll think of something, if you give me a minute. Gee, let me see, a selection of New York papers to start with – that's for Paw, he can't do without them." Her eyes strayed to his muscular arms with his shirt sleeves rolled up. "Say, are those real?"

She reached out and touched his arm inquisitively, just as the shop door opened again admitting the one person William had been waiting for with nervous anticipation.

Sally had not been looking forward to the visit, and had been rehearsing over and over again in her mind how to break the bad news she had just received from Clive about his book. The sudden shock of seeing Veronica and William in close proximity made her heart lurch in an unexpected manner. She halted and started to withdraw, feeling an unexpected twinge of jealousy.

"Sorry, I've just remembered something."

At the sight of her, William bounded forward eagerly. "Wait…" But Sally was gone.

He was about to dash after her when Hettie, seeing a potential order vanishing into thin air, hurried forward.

"William, remember our customer!"

But her entreaty fell on deaf ears.

"You'll have to excuse me." William was already tearing off his overall, ready to spring after Sally when Hettie wailed in desperation.

"William, you can't go yet." In a flash of inspiration, "I've got to go and see how your uncle is. I won't be long – don't forget it's Saturday," she emphasised, nodding significantly at Veronica, "we close at lunchtime."

"See here, if you don't want my business," Veronica uncoiled herself huffily.

His hand on the door, William turned back reluctantly. "Sorry, Hettie, off you go – I'll look after things until you get back. Right," he conjured up an apologetic smile, "what can we get you?"

Veronica relented. "Well, let me see." She reeled off a list of periodicals and groceries so fast William had to grab a pen and hastily scribble it all down in a rush to keep up with her. He managed to repeat it all back, and his efforts were rewarded by a beaming smile and thumbs up from Hettie as she left.

"Good boy," Veronica flashed a triumphant grin, confident she had got her way. "Now you just deliver those goodies after closing and I'll see if I can rustle up a drink or two. Byee."

While he was grappling in his mind how to go about dealing with such a large order, a head popped cautiously around the door and Sally, seeing the coast was clear, came back in.

"Has she gone?"

"Yes, thank heavens," agreed William, his face lighting up at the sight of her. "I hope we didn't put you off."

Putting her feelings behind her, Sally replied steadily, "No, of course not." She faced up to him bravely. "I managed to have a word with Clive, and …"

"Don't tell me," he interrupted glumly, seeing her expression. "He wasn't interested."

Sally's courage deserted her, and she added quickly, "He's promised to look at it." Taking in his harassed state, she decided to put off telling him for the moment, and changed the conversation. "I did tell your uncle I'd look in and see if I could help at all." She glanced around. "Is he all right? I can't see him anywhere."

"He's got himself crocked up, after that fight yesterday. The doctor's looking in later to see how he is."

"Oh, poor man, that means you're short of staff - anything I can do?" Seeing him hesitate, she added lightly, "Unless you're already fixed up. I see you're not short of admirers?"

William looked a trifle uncomfortable. "Oh, that was only Veronica – I thought she'd never go. She and her father have just moved in next door to Hettie. I was just trying to work out this order of hers," he waved helplessly at a wad of paper with a long list scribbled on it, and scratched his head. "She wants me to deliver this lot by lunchtime, and I don't know where to start." Seeing her questioning look, he explained, "Hettie's just popped out to see to uncle. She usually knows where everything is."

"Right," decided Sally practically. "I know, why don't you see to the papers while I sort out some of the groceries, and see how it goes?"

"Oh, would you - that would be great, are you sure?" he asked apologetically. "It's just that your mother didn't seem too keen on you staying yesterday."

"Don't worry about Ma, she's always blowing hot air – I've got Dad on my side, thank goodness. Here goes." She tore off half the sheet. "That's the newspapers and mags, I'll have a go at the rest. Let's see," she consulted the list.

"Cereal and soups to start with – I'll check the shelves over there. Ah, there they are, off we go."

The next half hour they worked alongside in companionable silence, stopping only to serve the regulars calling in who stopped to watch with great interest as they ticked off the items until they had a great pile stacked up on the floor.

"Well, that's terrific," enthused William, surveying the scene. "I don't know what I'd have done without your help. I'd have been here until midnight."

"Glad to be of help," smiled Sally, pushing back a stray lock of hair. "Whew, if you get that sort of order every week, you'll soon be in the money."

William brightened at the thought, relieved the immediate problem was solved. "Thank goodness that's over. We're one or two magazines short, but we can easily put them on order. Now, I'll just get this lot next door – there should be a truck around somewhere." He hesitated. "Could you possibly hang on while I get rid of this lot in case we get any more customers?"

"Of course, are you sure you can manage on your own?" Sally viewed the mounting order doubtfully.

"No problem," decided William firmly, hiding his doubts, "you just watch me."

Fishing out a small truck, William attacked the pile, storing the items one by one, while Sally helpfully passed up some of the more awkward bundles for him to stack.

At last, he stood back panting with a satisfied sigh. Then anxious for some excuse to see her again, he turned bashfully and shuffled his feet. "Look, can I offer you a drink or lunch at the pub later on when I get back, or have you got other plans?"

Conscious of his nearness, Sally laughed self-consciously. "That would be nice." She managed to resist a sudden impulse to smooth his face with a cooling touch. "Off you go. I'll keep an eye on things until Hettie gets back – and don't get too involved with that American gel, as Ma would say," she added impishly.

"Heaven forbid - that's the last thing I'd do," William assured her fervently. "Don't forget that lunch," he reminded her, buoyed up by the prospect. "I shan't be long."

"I'll be here, don't worry," she promised.

William's optimism was short lived. Arriving fully laden with supplies William was greeted by the sounds of dance music wafting out through the open windows and peals of laughter inside. Disconcerted by the noise, William misjudged the last few steps at the gate, and the hand truck developed a mind of its own, careering with increasing speed down the path towards the front door.

Inside, Ed Newman was feeling mildly irritated by his daughter's unexpected interest in William, and the lack of drinks did nothing to improve his temper.

"Say honey, I thought you said we were getting in some fresh supplies – where's my bourbon you promised?"

Veronica stopped twirling around, and faced her father soothingly. "Don't worry, Paw – it's on its way, trust me."

There was a sudden crash outside, followed by a splintering noise then silence.

"What the devil's that?" he protested.

Veronica placed a finger over her father's mouth to silence him. "Hush Paw, that'll be him." She fixed him with a daughter's eye that brooked no arguments. "I want you to be real nice to William - he's so dishy," she ended dreamy eyed. "Now you give him a drink the moment he gets here and make him welcome," she insisted, leaving no margin for error, "and don't forget our good old southern hospitality."

"What happened to Joe – you know, the one in the oil business?" Newman asked anxiously, following her to the door. "I thought you and he were all hunky dory."

"That's yesterday's news," Veronica threw over her shoulder. "Now you know you've never refused me anything I really wanted, Paw – just be nice to William."

"Ah, there you are," she called out, cutting off his grumbles. "Come in, oh," she stopped, eyeing piles of half open boxes strewn across the pathway. "What's happened?"

"It sort of got carried away," William offered sheepishly. "I'll, er, bring it in – where do you want it?"

"For Pete's sake," burst out her father, appearing at the doorway. "What d'you call this – looks like some kind of landslide."

"Now why don't you go and sit down, Paw," she insisted firmly, "while Willie and I round up the goodies." She made a motion of downing a drink. "And break out the drinks while you're at it to get us in the mood."

"But gee, honey, we haven't had anything to eat yet," he started to complain, then catching the full force of her commanding eye, subsided resignedly. "Just as you say, Vee."

A short while later he reappeared bearing a tray with glasses and a half empty bottle. He picked it up and regarded it in dismay. "Gee, don't say that's the last one." He seemed surprised at the discovery, forgetting he had already been putting in some hefty spadework on the existing supplies. "We sure need some more to keep us going. I know." Struck by a sudden idea, he grabbed the bottle and made for the kitchen, gleefully adding some water from the cold tap. "That should do it," he muttered. "A bit more, and that young man won't notice any difference." His optimism was short-lived, for just at that moment the tap gave a splutter and dried up.

"Holy smoke," he gritted. "Now what'll I do? I know, I'll try next door – bound to have some there."

Getting no answer from Hettie's, he carried on to Albert's cottage. Finding the door ajar, he pushed it open and after calling out without success tiptoed through into the kitchen. To his intense annoyance, the tap didn't seem to be working there either. "Jeepers, that's all I need," he despaired. He was about to give up when he caught sight of a bottle of what looked like mineral water on the kitchen dresser and his eyes lit up hopefully. He peered at the writing on the label and grunted. "Well, I guess he won't miss a tot or two, whoever Ferdie is. Well, here goes," and lifting the bottle in salute, he tilted it up and took an experimental swig.

As the thick cloying medicine hit the back of his throat, he spluttered and coughed, his face turning a bright red. "By Jimminy, that's the real McCoy," he gasped, fighting for breath. "That guy Ferdie sure knows a thing or two." He caught sight of a small medicine bottle next to it, and thoughtfully stuffed it in his pocket before leaving. "Gee, I might need some of that, in case I get a hangover," he decided, taking another generous swig from the bottle. As he made his way unsteadily back along the high street past the farmyard, the plaintive mooing of a cow caught his attention, and he reacted to the mournful gaze sympathetically. "Here, I guess your need is greater than mine," he said, fumbling in his pocket. His attempts at getting the bottle out stalled, so he decided the right and decent thing to do would be to deliver it personally.

Clambering with some difficulty over the stone wall, he staggered across the yard and finally succeeded in lobbing the medicine bottle into the enclosure. Swaying with the effort, he stumbled a few more steps before the accumulated effects of Ferdie's medicine, coming on top of his earlier substantial intake of whisky on an empty stomach, proved the final straw and he sank into a bed of hay in the corner of the farmyard still clutching his booty and passed out, a blissful smile on his lips.

Back in the cottage, making the most of her opportunity, Veronica led William to a deckchair and pouring out a generous helping of whisky into a glass, pressed it into his hand. "Go on, drink up – you deserve it, Willie boy."

Thankfully, William did as he was told, and although not achieving the same unusual results as her father, he lay back exhausted. And it was not until he heard the Church clock chime the hour that he remembered his date with Sally.

Looking at his watch, he exclaimed in a stupor, "Oh no, is that the time?"

"Say, what's the hurry – just as we were getting to know each other?" drawled Veronica, settling herself down next to him, and running her fingers through his hair.

"You don't understand," he groaned, staggering to his feet. "I've got to get back to the shop. I promised to see someone."

"Who's that – not that stuck up limey friend of yours?"

"She's not stuck up," defended William hotly, then remembering he had just landed a large order thanks entirely to his hostess, he exclaimed hurriedly. "It's not that, it's the shop. My gosh, it's early closing and there's nobody there to cash up, and poor old Hettie's trying to look after

Albert at the same time." He was halfway out of the cottage before he remembered to make his apologies.

"Thanks for the order," he babbled, "and all your help – it will make Albert buck up no end." He hesitated awkwardly. "Perhaps we can return the favour some time."

After his footsteps died away Veronica downed the rest of her drink, and heaved herself up. "Big deal."

Just as he feared, when he got back to the shop William found it empty, except for a terse note, the contents of which made him groan in frustration. It read: 'Stayed till shop closed. Came back to remind you, but saw you were busy with Veronica – so I'm having lunch with Clive.'

As the words danced in front of his eyes, his befuddled gaze finally concentrated on the heavily underlined word and he stifled a curse. He was still cursing to himself when Hettie burst into the shop a few minutes later and clung to the doorway.

"Oh, William," she moaned, "you'll never guess."

"I know." He thrust the note in his pocket. "She's given me the bird."

"Talk sense," she said feverishly, "it's not the bird – it's the cow. It's Ferdie."

William rallied and tried to get a grip on things, conscious that he was losing the thread of the conversation. "What are you talking about?"

"I'm trying to tell you," Hettie repeated with a wail. "Someone's had Ferdie's medicine, and given Albert's tonic to the cow!"

Chapter Five
The Break-in

It was a thoroughly dispirited William who made his way to the shop next morning, with his Aunt's message, 'Don't forget to ask about your wages', still ringing in his ears.

Inside, he found a small crowd of customers gathered around Hettie who was getting flustered about the questions she was being asked.

"Yes, yes, we're doing all right, I assure you," she was telling Ted. "Ah, there you are, William. He'll be able to fill you in. Now, who's next?"

"So, what's all this, squire?" Ted cocked an eye as he rolled his cigarette expertly with one hand. "Coming up in the world are we, with all these new orders from overseas? They won't like it, will they – Foxy Fred and that lot?"

"I don't see why?" said William distractedly, his mind still on what he would say to Sally when he met her again. As he turned to see outside all thoughts of what Ted was trying to warn him about abruptly vanished at the sight that met his gaze, and he dashed outside just in time to see Sally getting into a car across the road.

"Hi, Sally, wait - I must talk to you. Hang on…"

"Sorry, can't stop," said Sally looking ahead, smiling brightly, hiding an aching heart. "Clive's taking me out for the day."

"I'm sorry about yesterday," went on William desperately, trying to get her to listen. "I can explain everything." But his words were lost in the roar of the exhaust as Clive leaned out jeering, as he revved up.

"Out of the way, old chap, can't keep the lady waiting…oh, and I believe this is yours…catch!" As the car moved off, William saw Sally arguing with Clive, who grabbed a package and tossed it out of the car as it gathered speed.

Bending down, William saw it was a battered parcel containing his stories. He stood there for a while sick at heart, watching the car disappear up the street, then he turned dejectedly and went back into the store.

As he entered, Ted was collecting his change. Seeing William, he advised, "I should keep an eye on that Clive. I wouldn't trust him if I were you -

and as for those characters hanging around outside," he nodded at the doorway, "I should watch 'em an' all. Up to no good, you mark my words," and hoisting up his bag he went out, humming a tune.

Handing over change to the last customer left in the queue Hettie peeled off her overall as she came out from behind the counter. "Good, take over, William, there's a dear. I must go and see how Albert is. Oh, and I'll take this cash and get him to pay some of the bills," she decided, emptying the till. "You've no idea how it's mounting up. Shan't be long. You'll be all right for a bit, won't you. I don't suppose we'll get anyone else in now – they'll all be reading their Sunday newspapers, or off to Church."

"Of course," agreed William, peering out of the window to see who Ted had been talking about. All he could see were a couple of youths leaning against a car, apparently chatting to someone on their mobile. Just as he was watching, an old man dressed like a tramp approached and entered the shop, and he forgot all about them.

"Can I help you?" William offered, but the man mumbled, "Just looking," and shuffled round the back, casting a quick look now and then in William's direction.

William nodded and picked up a paper at random for something to do. After a cursory glance at the headlines, he sat back and let his thoughts wander, concentrating his mind on Sally and wondering miserably what he could do to put things right between them.

He was interrupted from his musings by the shop bell tinkling, and the two youths entered and took a swift look around. Reassured, they pulled a scarf up over their faces and advanced menacingly towards the counter.

William came out of his daydream and sat up blinking, as the nearest one pulled out a pistol and pointed it at his head.

"Where's the cash, mate? No tricks mind, don't move – watch him, Smudge," as William instinctively reached under the counter for the panic button.

Sensing his move, Jed waved his gun and shouted, "Quick, stop him, yer fool!"

"Right ho, Jed." The spotty youth lunged obediently with a cosh, sending William sprawling with a glancing blow. Dazed, he shook his head groggily and grabbed at the counter for support. Then things began to happen all at once, with a surprising turn of speed.

Hearing the threatening voices, the old man straightened up in the background and called out with an authoritative voice, "Stop that, you young devils, d'you hear?"

Jed spared him a brief contemptuous glance. "Belt up granddad, or you'll catch a load of the same medicine."

"No," answered the old man with unexpected spirit, "you catch it." And picking up an empty crate, he heaved it at him defiantly.

Caught off guard, the one called Jed flung up an arm instinctively and the gun went off, shattering a bottle on the shelf and at the same time reducing the spotty one to a nervous wreck.

Seizing the opportunity, William picked up the nearest objects to hand and started hurling them at the intruders, and in seconds the air was full of whizzing missiles.

"Jed, let's get out of here," gulped the spotty one nervously, backing to the door.

Whatever Jed was going to say was cut off as the old man picked up another crate and brought it down on his head.

Put off his stroke, the leader staggered off balance and decided he'd had enough. Searching around dazedly for some spoils to take with them, he yelled, "Grab those cigarettes," and swinging his gun around wildly he retreated yelling, "and keep back both of you!"

The next moment there was a totally bizarre interruption and his words went unheeded. The door opened and a weird shape appeared in the doorway freezing everyone's attention like the action of a slow motion film grinding to a halt.

Only a short while earlier, Ed Newman had begun to wake up in Hettie's backyard, feeling wet and bleary eyed. Focusing his gaze with an effort, he found himself gazing up stupidly at the looming shape of a pig, peering down at him with friendly curiosity. Hastily inching himself away as fast as he could in the slithering mud, he hauled himself up and squelched through the clinging ooze of the pig sty and out of the stable yard into the High Street. Unable to see clearly, he felt his way along the wall until his hand came into contact with a door handle, and he pushed his way in, calling out feebly for assistance.

As he tottered into the shop uttering a string of wild croaks and snorting sounds, reminiscent of the farmyard he had just vacated, and covered head to foot in mud and slime, his appearance had a paralysing effect on the intruders. The one in command called Jed stood there for a split second, his mouth wide open, then the gun dropped from his nerveless fingers and he made a rapid bolt for the door, followed closely by the spotty one who dropped the cigarette packets in a panic, spilling them all over the floor.

William sat down with a thump to get his breath back, and started to stammer his thanks to his elderly rescuer, quite forgetting the gory spectacle of Newman, who slowly sank to the floor. "You were great - don't know what I'd have done if you hadn't been there."

The old man came forward modestly. "Glad to be of help, my boy. I think we put paid to their little game." He eyed William. "My word, you've got a nasty gash over that eye. We'd better get you to a doctor."

Shrugging off his concern, William heaved himself up and dabbed his face with his handkerchief. "No, can't afford to leave the shop just now – there's nobody to take over."

"Well, in that case," the old man pulled a mobile out of his baggy overcoat. "I'll get my girl along – we need someone with a level head." Pressing a few buttons, he held it gingerly to his ear and spoke gruffly to someone at the other end. "That you, my darling? Where are you? Right. I'm at the village shop – there's been a break-in. Yes, it's a young man – had a nasty accident. Can you spare a minute?" Shoving it back in his pocket, he looked satisfied. "That should keep them happy."

Answering William's look of enquiry, he grumbled. "Can't stand this modern technology – not my idea. It's Margery's - always on at me. Seems to think I can't be trusted to go anywhere without one of these blessed mobile things. That's women for you, they're all the same. Take that daughter of mine. Normally quite a sensible level headed girl, but she's got herself involved with some nincompoop I wouldn't give you tuppence for – all because of some silly upset with her boyfriend. What would you do with them?"

His eloquence sparked off a hidden feeling of grievance that had been festering in William's heart all morning. "Don't talk to me about girls," he said moodily, dabbing at his face. "I've given up trying to understand them. Just because I was trying to help a customer..."

"Here," the old man interrupted, handed over a handkerchief, "try this one. Now," he glanced around the shop, "have you got such a thing as a first aid kit?"

"I tell you, I'm all right." William attempted to change the subject. "Look, the shop's in a mess. I must try to tidy up before Hettie gets back, or I'll be in trouble. It's very good of you, but..."

"Now, don't be a silly ass," reproved the old man. "Look, the blood is dripping all over you." He placed a restraining hand on William, "Don't worry, Sally will be here in a minute, she's been on a first aid course - she'll look after you. Meanwhile, I'll have a quick scout around for that first aid kit."

At the mention of Sally's name, William shook his head and made a determined effort to get up.

"I don't want any female looking after me, honestly."

At that moment, the bell tinkled frantically at the shop door and Sally rushed in. At the sight of William amidst the chaos, his face streaked in blood, she flung herself at him wailing. "Oh, darling – what have they done to you?"

William's mouth opened and closed like a goldfish. "Did…did you say, 'darling'? He swallowed. "I only asked because the last time I saw you…"

"I know, I know, will you ever forgive me?" Over her shoulder, she called out, "Daddy, bring some water and a towel – there's a tap by the back door."

She knelt in front of him, and raising her head gazed up at William, pleading, "I waited and waited and when you didn't turn up I came looking for you, and she was cosying up to you, I thought…I don't know what I thought. Then Clive turned up and kept on nagging at me to go out with him, I never dreamed he would be so awful."

"What happened?" asked William, fascinated.

"Yes, what did he do?" demanded her father, bristling in the background.

"Well, after he threw your stories out of the car, I ticked him off, and he laughed so much he nearly drove us into the ditch. I think he must have been drunk," she added, trying to explain his behaviour.

"Go on."

"Well, he kept on boasting about his beastly business, and how he had Ma's blessing, and then he had the cheek to stop the car and tried to kiss me." She wiped the back of her hand across her mouth, as if to wipe away the memory.

"What?" William's face darkened.

"You wouldn't make me marry that man, would you, Daddy?" Sally asked her father, as he handed over a bowl of water.

"Of course not, the blighter," thundered her father, nearly spilling the water.

"Not even if Ma insisted?"

"Well, um, no, of course not… hem." Her father hesitated. "I'm sure your mother will see sense…eventually. Here, you need this," he added lamely, handing over a towel.

"Good," Sally heaved a sigh of relief and looked up at William shyly. "I'm still waiting to be asked."

William blinked and gulped. "You mean... you mean?"

For an answer, she pulled his face down towards her.

"Does that mean?" He tilted up her face, and after seeing her expression showered her with kisses with wild delight. After a long pause and some coughing in the background, William looked up apologetically.

"I hope you don't mind, sir?"

"Don't mind me, go right ahead, my boy."

Without wasting any more time, William did as he was told, and clasped her to him again. "Mmm, I've been wanting to do that ever since I first saw you."

"Well, there's nothing stopping you now, is there darling?" she said happily, snuggling up close again.

There was a sudden interruption that proved an exception to the rule. The shop door was flung open for the second time that morning and Veronica rushed in, peering around in a distraught fashion.

"Have you seen my Paw?" Then catching sight of the inert shape on the floor, she burst out, "Jeepers, what have you done to him?" and flinging herself down on the floor, tried to raise his head.

"Paw, say something."

Newman's eyes tried to focus on her and he smiled weakly. With an effort he propped himself up on one elbow and looked around owlishly. "Say, that was a helluva nightcap. What was it called?" He searched around in his mind. "Never mind...it'll come to me...hic."

"Paw, you're drunk," she hissed. Casting a scornful look at the happy smile on William's face, she exploded, "Fine friend you turned out to be. Someone give me a hand." She took in Sally's father. "Get that old man to help me, if you're so busy."

"Of course." Sally's father stepped forward gallantly. "Allow me, my dear. William, if you could take hold of his legs, I'm sure we can manage."

"Of course." William came out of a trance and let Sally go reluctantly.

Conscious of Veronica's seething fury, the old man explained as they lifted him up, "I'm afraid you must think it all very odd, my dear. But I'm afraid we've had a break in, and your father came in just at a critical moment and helped to frighten them off. We're all very grateful, isn't that right, my boy?"

Catching his eye, William agreed hastily. "Yes, of course. He was great."

They stopped at the door. "If you could do the honours, my dear," the old man asked Veronica courteously.

His request went unanswered, for at that moment the door opened and Hettie breezed in, then stopped short in horrified amazement at the scene of utter destruction.

Her sudden appearance caused William to loosen his grip, and Newman staggered to his feet and stood swaying there with a dreamy look on his face.

"What on earth's been going on?" asked Hettie bewildered, then seeing Newman's condition, and not recognising him under the coating of mud, made the pardonable mistake of thinking him responsible. "Well really!" she gasped indignantly, "How did he get in here – and what sort of behaviour do you call this?"

It was the final straw for his daughter Veronica. Stepping forward, she seethed with rage, "You have the darn nerve to suggest my Paw did all this? Well, lemme tell you, that does it."

With a gulp of recognition, Hettie pleaded, "Wait, there must be some sort of mistake. I didn't realise it was you, Veronica dear, please forgive me."

But Veronica was in no mood to forgive anyone – her fighting blood was up.

Paraphrasing the immortal spirit of Lady Courtney, as she helped her father leave, she hissed, "I'll have you know, in future, we'll take our custom elsewhere." As a parting shot, she added for William's benefit, "And there was I thinking we were getting to know each other real well. Come on, Paw."

As the door closed behind them, William and Sally and her father tried to explain to Hettie what had occurred. Amid the babble of voices, a lone and plaintive voice did its best to make itself heard.

"I say, what's all this – stocktaking?" Albert stood at the back door, peering somewhat fearfully at the gathering. He pottered in, still in his dressing gown, trying to make sense of the sight that met his eyes. Seeing everyone struck dumb at his appearance, Albert rambled on, "Ah, I see we have company – Sir Henry and Miss Sally, how good of you to look in. Excuse me for not dressing, but I have not been very well, you understand."

Gathering Sally close to him, William tried to gather his scattered wits. "I'm sorry it's all been a bit hectic here, Uncle."

Memory of recent events brought a pleased smile to Albert's face. "You don't have to apologise, my boy. I hear we have to congratulate you, William, for putting the shop back on its feet again, with that splendid order from our American friends." He heaved a sigh of relief. "I don't mind telling you I was beginning to lose heart at the way things were going, but now we're on the mend at last, thank goodness."

"Oh, Albert," Hettie fussed over him, after an awkward pause. "You should have stayed in bed. Why don't you go up and I'll bring you a hot drink and tell you all about it?"

Sir Henry looked embarrassed. "I think we'd better leave you good people in peace to sort things out between you. Good Lord, is that the time – I must be off. Oh, I nearly forgot what I came in for – have you got my usual baccy? That's it, on the top shelf, I think."

Feverishly, William combed the shelves until he came up with the one Sally's father wanted. He waited patiently at the till as Sir Henry went through his pockets and came out empty handed.

"Dash it, I don't seem to have the ready. Sally pet, can you oblige?"

Sighing, Sally opened her purse and shook it regretfully. "Sorry, Dad, I seem to have come out without any. William love, how are you fixed?"

Seeing his hesitation, Hettie dived into her purse and produced a note hastily, "There you are William, take this." She laughed nervously. "Silly me, we quite forgot to give you your wages this week, didn't we, Mr Bridge?"

Albert coughed. "Yes, very remiss of us, I'm sure. Remind me to give you a bonus for your sterling work yesterday."

The note changed hands, finally reaching Sir Henry. He handed it back in turn to William, beaming, "There you are, let me see, does that cover it?"

"Of course, sir," agreed William automatically. He rang the amount up on the till and searched the compartments. "Sorry, there doesn't seem to be any small change."

"Never mind, my boy, pay me next time you see me," said Sir Henry absentmindedly, pocketing his tobacco. Then hearing his mobile shrill, he picked it up cautiously and listened with an occasional, "Yes, my dear, certainly, my dear," before replacing it, as if expecting it to explode at any minute. "That was your mother," he explained, just to make it crystal clear. Checking his watch, he said hastily, "My word, is that the time? Come along, Sally, or we'll be late for our guests." Then remembering his manners, he made his hurried farewells. "Well, goodbye William - so pleased we've got you young people back together again."

"Coming Pa," obliged Sally dutifully, planting a passing kiss on William's forehead. "Now, no more gallivanting, my precious – promise me."

"You have my word," said William fervently. "Never again."

"Ah well," pronounced Albert, as William dreamily shut the empty till after they had gone, "we mustn't spoil the ship for a ha'penny worth of tar, must we? Never mind," he beamed, "things are looking up at last, eh?"

Following a pregnant silence, Hettie took Albert's arm and led him away anxiously, trying to think of the best way of breaking the news. "Come along, Albert, there's something I need to tell you."

"Yes, in a minute, Hettie – after I've checked the post."

Left alone, William sat back putting off the job of clearing up and let his mind dwell lovingly on Sally. He would have stayed there for the rest of the morning, had not the door burst open again and Albert reappeared distraught, waving a letter in his hand.

"D'you know what? She's going to get married!"

"I know – I can't believe it," William said blissfully.

"Did you know about this?" cried Albert in anguish.

"Well, I haven't actually asked her yet, but I'm hoping Sally will say 'yes'," agreed William, his thoughts dwelling happily on the prospect.

"Miss Sally? Who told her – am I the last one to hear about it?" Albert clutched his head and read the letter in his hand again to make sure. "She says here she's not coming back – she getting married next week."

"Next week - as soon as that?" William came out of his rosy dream with a start and marvelled. "Are you sure? I didn't know we'd got that far."

At the sound of their voices, Hettie appeared and tried to calm Albert down. "I think your uncle's talking about Jackie, his assistant."

"But what am I to do?" groaned Albert. "We can't go on like this, staggering from one crisis to another. If it wasn't for that order of Newman's, we'd be right in the soup."

William looked at Hettie who shook her head anxiously, entreating him not to say any more.

"Why don't you come and lie down and rest, Albert dear," she said coaxingly, "while young William and I put our heads together and see if we can think of something."

"I don't see how," despaired Albert, allowing himself to be led away. "Without Jackie to help me, I'll just have to sell up."

Chapter Six
Help Is At Hand

It was a sombre Hettie who returned about half an hour later. She sank into the nearest seat, looking utterly crushed. "What are we going to do to get us out of this mess?"

"It's going to need a miracle," agreed William, reluctantly tearing himself away from his private dreams. "Isn't there anyone we know who could help?" As he spoke, he mentally ran through a list of his friends on the paper where he had worked and after a fruitless search gave up reluctantly. "No, if word gets around, it wouldn't do us much good. There must be someone, somewhere who would be willing to give a hand. An old friend of the family perhaps, although I can't think of anyone offhand."

Hettie sat up with a jerk. "Of course, why didn't I think of it before – Albert's brother, of course."

William looked puzzled. "His brother – I didn't know he had another one, apart from Dad? He's never mentioned it to me."

"Oh, yes." Hettie was definite on that point. "I asked him the other day about him and I got the impression he didn't want to bother him." She hesitated and chose her words tactfully. "I wondered at the time - the way he talked about him - whether he was some kind of ... black sheep of the family, if you know what I mean." She searched her memory. "His name was Neil, I think he said." Her voice sounded doubtful.

"Well, there's only one way to find out – why don't we ask him?"

"We can't ask Albert just now." Hettie sounded shocked. "He's in such a state."

"Hasn't he got a phone list somewhere?" William asked patiently. "We could look this chap Neil up – he can only say 'no' – what have we got to lose?"

"I suppose so," Hettie yielded a point. "I don't like to look through his things though without him knowing, but I suppose it's an emergency."

"You could say that," agreed William with feeling.

Hettie got to her feet, her mind made up. "Right, you stay here while I find out. If I don't have any luck I suppose we ought to ring the police, and let them know what's happened about the break-in. Don't touch anything in case they need it for evidence," she added in passing, remembering vaguely of the way they dealt with such matters in the recent detective series she'd seen on TV.

William gave a derisive snort. "Fat chance they'll find anything with all the people we've had going through the place."

Within minutes she was back with a squeal of excitement. "You'll never guess, here it is. Look - Neil Bridge, I was right after all." She hesitated. "Will you ring him, or shall I?"

"You ring him." William was quite firm. "When I was on the local rag, we always got one of the women reporters to phone up when we wanted an interview – they always sound more appealing. It's a dead cert."

As she hesitated, William encouraged, "Go on, I'll listen on the extension. You can always pass him over."

With some trepidation, Hettie rang the number and was taken aback when a voice barked impatiently, "Yes, who's that?"

As Hettie began to explain, there was a sudden guffaw at the other end, and a voice hooted, "Old Albert in trouble? I don't believe it. Cor blimey. That's one for the book."

Then at the sound of a wailing police siren in the background, they heard a hurried aside to someone, and the voice came back in a hurry. "Listen, tell Albert I'll be down as soon I can shake the rozzers off. Don't worry, love." And with that the line went dead.

Hettie and William looked at each other in wild surmise, as they both slowly replaced their receivers.

"What d'you make of that?" Hettie asked bewildered, and William shook his head, equally puzzled.

"Sounds as if the police were after him," he said half disbelieving.

"Look out," warned Hettie, "talking about the police."

A helmet appeared around the shop door, followed by the substantial presence of Constable

Cuthbert, the local bobby. At the sight of the mess on the floor he whistled.

"So he wasn't having me on, after all. Sorry Miss Hettie and young William, sir, I thought they were pulling my leg back at the office. Whew, what's happened here?"

As they both tried to explain at once, the policeman held up his hand. "One at a time, if you don't mind."

"I think you'd better ask William here – he was here when it happened. He knows all about it."

"Right." He got out his notebook and licked a pencil. "When you're ready, sir," he broke off at the sound of his mobile. "Oh, excuse me. Yes? No, not now, I'm busy. What was that? Well, keep me posted, you know where I am."

He put his mobile away. "Sorry about that, sir, some trouble about a prisoner escaping up in the sticks – someone else can deal with that for the time being. Now sir, perhaps you can explain what happened while I examine the scene of the crime, as it were."

As William's recital came to an end, Constable Cuthbert put his notebook away, and turned the information over in his mind, "He called him

'Jed' did he? And the other one was 'Smudge', you say?" He nodded ponderously. "I think we've come across those villains before – a couple of tearaways, from what I remember. Now if you can give me a description, sir, I'll see we get a radio warning out in case they try the same thing somewhere else." He broke off again, plainly irritated by his mobile, just as William opened his mouth to answer. "Yes, what is it this time? What? He's said to be heading this way? What does he look like?"

The constable turned to William apologetically, just as a head appeared at the window behind him and tried to attract their attention. At the sight of the policeman, there was a muffled gasp, and the head quickly dropped down out of sight again.

"If you'll excuse me, sir, I'll be off. There seems to be something up at the moment."

He turned to go. "I'll be in touch."

Directly the shop door closed behind him, there was a tap at the side door, and a tousled head appeared around the corner. Satisfied the coast was clear, the rest of the body followed, accompanied by a curious rattling noise.

"Has he gone? Good, excuse me while I get rid of this contraption."

In answer to their look of surprise, he announced in quick bursts. "Oh, I'm Neil, in case you hadn't guessed. Excuse me while I get this thing off. Ah, that's better." He wrenched a metal tag off his ankle. "Couldn't get here any speedier with this blasted thing clogging up the works." He grinned boyishly, looking suddenly more like an overgrown teenager caught in a schoolboy prank. "You must be Hettie. Hi."

"Hello," said Hettie faintly. "Aren't you supposed to keep that…thing on?"

"What - this?" Neil held it up for inspection. "So they can keep tabs on me all the time? Not on your Nelly." He tossed it to William, who automatically caught it.

"Here, you can look after that. I should get rid of it pronto – the village duck pond will do – while Hettie puts me in the picture."

As William was about to object, he caught an anxious look of appeal from Hettie and decided the sooner he disposed of it the better, what with the thought of the village bobby in the neighbourhood, and about to return at any moment.

No sooner had he stepped outside when a car with a blue light flashing pulled up alongside, and the uniformed driver inside hailed him.

"Excuse me, sir."

Trying to calm the thumping noise his heart was making, William walking nervously around to the driver's side and bent down at the half open window, hurriedly hiding the incriminating evidence behind his back.

"Have you seen any strangers around here lately?"

William considered the remark and answered carefully, hoping to hide the tremor in his voice. "No, only family, you know."

"Nobody wandering around just now with a metal tag around his ankle?"

Pressing the object in question even closer behind his back, he answered truthfully, "Not now, no."

"Right, sir. Well, in that case, Jeffrey you'd better get out and keep your eyes open," he called over his shoulder.

Stepping back hurriedly, William opened the rear door for the other constable who proceeded to clamber out with some difficulty. As the constable straightened up in front of him William seized the opportunity and dropped the metal tag on the back seat, shutting the door before the constable had a chance to turn around.

Wiping the nervous sweat from his forehead he waved away the driver with as much cheerfulness as he could muster and returned to the shop, conscious of a great weight lifted from his shoulders.

Inside, only heavy breathing could be heard, until one by one, first Hettie's head appeared from next door, then after a pause Neil emerged behind her.

"Well?" he questioned eagerly, "was that the rozzers?"

Feeling weak around the knees, William steadied himself on the counter while he related what had happened.

"Why, that's great! Good for you, young Willie. I can call you that, can't I?"

William nodded wordlessly. Although ready for a game of sport with the best of them, he was suddenly aware with a shiver what he had just done.

"They'll know it was me, directly they look in the back," he uttered nervously.

Neil joked, "Don't worry, I'll come and see you on visitors' days. Seriously," he said dismissing William's fears with a light laugh, "as far as they're concerned, it could have been anyone." He placed a friendly arm around his nephew. "If I know anything, it'll be back in the lost property before any questions are asked. More to the point," he pondered, "what I need to know right now is – how am I going to disguise myself while we sort out this problem of yours?" He gazed at them in turn, sizing them up. "Now, Hettie, you're about my size. What have you got in that wardrobe next door to turn me into a fairy godmother?"

Hettie regarded him open-mouthed, before dissolving into giggles.

Before she could answer, they heard a knock at the shop door and the authoritative voice of Constable Cuthbert was heard outside. Thinking quickly, Hettie seized hold of Neil and hustled him away, whispering, "Quick, get rid of him, Willie love."

Recovering from a feeling of impending doom, William croaked, "Come in."

"Ah, Officer, what can we do for you?" he said quickly, trying to keep the hysterical note out of his voice. "They're all out at the moment - can I help?"

"If you don't mind, sir," Constable Cuthbert moved majestically into the shop. "I'd like to run over those details again, just to make sure like."

"Details?" echoed William, his mind still grappling with thoughts of his recent act of folly.

"Yes, sir." The constable proceeded to mark out the area with a piece of chalk on his hands and knees, ending up at the back door to Albert's quarters. "Hello, where does this lead to?" He scrambled to his feet, and started to open the door inquisitively.

"No, not that door," protested William thoroughly alarmed, closing his eyes and instinctively fearing the worst. When he opened them again, his eyes widened to golf ball size at the sight that met his gaze. There framed in the doorway was Neil heavily disguised under a flowing dress and elaborate wig that sat slightly askew on his head, nonchalantly smoking a cigarette in a long holder, with Hettie all of a twitter in the background.

"Do introduce me to this charming man," Neil commanded majestically in a falsetto voice.

William nearly spoiled it all by burying his face in a handkerchief, and started coughing instead. "This…this is my…my…"

"Aunt Isobel." Neil finished the sentence for him with a dramatic flourish of his cigarette holder.

"Aunt Isobel, of course," burbled William. "All the way from…"

"Brighton, on a family visit."

William grabbed at the lifeline. "As you can see, Officer, we are in the middle of a family reunion, so if you'll excuse us."

"Of course, sir and - madam?" The constable hesitated, turning to Neil. "Some other time then…pleased to make your acquaintance, m'am." He stood there bashfully twiddling his buttons, showing no sign of leaving, and appearing captivated by the sight of Aunt Isobel.

"My pleasure, Constable…?"

"Cuthbert, m'am, at your service." He fished some tickets out of his pocket. "Meanwhile, perhaps I might be so bold as to ask if you would be interested in buying tickets for our next village social – with some old fashioned dancing, I believe?"

"How kind. Oh, I seem to have left my purse next door. I'm a little out of practice these days, I'm afraid," she cooed. "Some other time perhaps."

"If you pardon my saying so, m'am, I'm sure you'd be the belle of the ball," insisted the constable with doglike devotion.

"Go on, you naughty man." Aunt Isobel gave him a playful push that sent him half flying across the room, nearly landing him on his back.

The unexpected assault only served to make the constable more enamoured than ever. Picking himself up, he straightened his uniform and cast a last bashful glance, before taking his leave. "The Ball won't be the same without you, Aunt Isobel m'am, if you'll pardon the expression – I'll call again sometime, in case you change your mind," he promised.

There was a fraught silence mingled with relief after his going, before William gave vent to his feelings. "Wow, that was a close shave."

Hettie silently agreed with him, but Neil would have none of it.

"Nonsense, it just shows what you can do when you try – and I wasn't even trying," he offered modestly. "Now, down to business." He became brisk. "Hettie has told me what's been happening, and it seems to me we should be more pro-active."

"More - what?"

"Pro-active," explained Neil patiently. "It's one of those PR gimmicks they use, that means we should be seen to be doing something more positive than just going along with the flow – as we appear to be doing now. Let's face it, there hasn't been much of that around here lately, has there, me old china?"

William was privately forced to agree, although he could see Hettie protesting in the background, out of loyalty to Albert.

"Yes, that might be true," he admitted, "but how do we go about it?"

"Well then, we need to get some action round here, and this is how I see it." Neil nodded several times as if endorsing his own opinion, while the others looked at him hopefully.

"First of all, we've got to concentrate on mending fences with this next door geezer of yours – Newman, or whatever his name is. He's the one with the loola to put you back on your plates of meat."

"On your – what?" repeated Hettie, mystified.

"Plates of meat – feet," explained Neil impatiently.

"That's pretty obvious, but how?" asked William glumly.

"What else can we do, if that doesn't work?" Hettie wanted to know.

"We'll just have to make sure it does work, won't we, eh?" said Neil briskly. "Meanwhile, we need to think ahead like, and drum up some bright ideas to bring the crowds in regular like – that will give us the bread and butter money, to keep us going."

Seeing their blank looks of disbelief, he ploughed on, "Anyway, the more immediate problem, as I see it, is how to get back into their good books next door – they're the ones with the loolah. Now, who do we know who gets on with them really well?"

Hettie brightened immediately. "Why, William here, of course. His daughter, Veronica, sort of took to you at first sight, didn't she, love?"

William shuddered. "Don't talk to me about that vampire. I'll never hear the last about it from Sally, if I have anything more to do with her."

"But think of Albert, dear. You want to do your best help him, don't you?"

"Yes, of course, but..." William shivered at the thought of the consequences.

Neil put it more bluntly. "Well, if you don't help out, chum, it's kaput - as far as I can see. Albert's had it."

"Just tell her you're sorry for all the upset - that's all you need to do, love," Hettie wheedled. "Surely you can do that for your uncle, can't you?"

"But I promised Sally I'd never have anything more to do with her." William looked from one to the other, appalled at the thought.

"I tell you what." Hettie was struck by a sudden thought. "Why don't we just invite them around for a cosy little supper, to get to know them better – that means we can keep it a private family invite, and not tell anyone else about it. How would that do?"

William considered the idea unhappily, aghast at the thought of concealing anything from Sally. "I know we need to keep up with them from a business point of view," he conceded reluctantly, "but I don't like the idea of ..."

"Good, that's settled then," ruled Neil. "I tell you what, young William, you pop next door and have a word with this Newman geezer, and say it's an old village custom to invite a new neighbour in for a nosh up. Tell him it's a well known British tradition."

"What – now?" said William desperately.

"No time like the present," answered Neil blandly.

William shot a final look of appeal at Hettie who nodded encouragingly. Dejectedly, he got up with a deep sigh, and made for the door.

"Oh, and don't forget," Neil called after him. "Tell him we've got his favourite Bourbon laid on - that should do the trick. Blimey, it would me."

In adding the after thought about the liquid refreshments, Neil had hit the nail well and truly on the head.

Ed Newman's eyes lit up ecstatically at the opportunity, as soon as their visitor had left.

"Yessir, we'll be there – in fact we'd be honoured to attend – you bet," he rapsodied, smacking his lips at the prospect ahead. "Yessir, we'll be there, won't we, Vee?"

To his astonishment, Veronica dug her highly polished heels in. "If you think I'm going to swop polite talk with those stuck-up Britishers, you've got another think coming, Paw."

"But, Vee honey, I thought you were all over that young, William – what's changed your mind?" Her father shook his head in bewilderment.

"Because he's two-timed me with that Courtney girl – he treated me like a dumb brick, that's what. Nobody messes with me, I'm telling you."

Newman squared his shoulders resolutely at the thought of all that Bourbon going to waste. "Well, I guess I'll just have to go and bat for the side on my own some," he said bravely. "We gotta be sociable now we're here, or we'll give the old U.S of A a bad name. But say, what darned excuse do I give them for you not being there?"

"Tell them I'm washing my hair – tell them anything you flaming well like, I don't care," she snapped, and slammed out of the room.

Her father picked up a pen hesitantly, and started writing. 'Dear Mr Bridge, I was delighted to receive your very kind invitation.' He scratched his head, 'Unfortunately, due to a prior engagement, my daughter…'

Meanwhile, over in Courtney Towers, Sally was facing up to a barrage of criticism from her stepmother, Lady Courtney, after word had leaked out about the raid on the village shop, and her subsequent reconciliation with William.

"Your father tells me," she began grimly, "that despite my…our strict instructions," she corrected frostily, "you deliberately flouted our wishes and engaged in a sordid act of flirtation with that young man, William Bridge, at the village shop. Oh, the humiliation of it all. How can I hold my head up at the next Women's Forum meeting?"

Sally stifled an immediate retort that sprang to mind, and replied in a placating tone, "Why, Ma, I was only treating a cut on that poor man after those men attacked the shop and knocked him out. Ask Dad – he was there helping William fight them off – he'll tell you."

Lady Courtney snorted. "I have already heard an account of the unseemly conduct of the affair from your father," refraining from adding that Sir Henry was still suffering from shock after the exchange, far more bruising than anything he had encountered in his battle with the shop intruders.

"Furthermore, I am shocked at the way you behaved towards Clive, when out of the goodness of his heart he offered to take you out to lunch after the disgraceful way that Bridge boy treated you, when all the time he was making advances at that sweet little girl, Veronica. What am I to say to Ed-ward when I see him?"

Stung out of her normal patience, Sally retorted, "If you really want to know how your precious Clive behaved, I'll have you know he was practically drunk and made a pass at me, and as for that sweet little Veronica, she was making all the advances – I had it all from William, and furthermore I'll have you know – we're engaged!"

After recovering from the shock, Lady Courtney said acidly, "Don't talk nonsense. Clive comes from a pedigree family and is a perfect gentleman – you probably upset him when he turned down those ridiculous stories that William was trying to get published – as if anyone would." Seeing Sally taken aback, she pressed home her attack. "And as for being engaged - if that was true, why is it that your so-called boyfriend has since invited Veronica and her father for a cosy supper – so I've just heard from Ed-ward," she sniffed. "Sounds to me like another opportunity for that young wastrel to make further amorous advances to that poor girl."

"That's not true, and I'll prove it," flared Sally defensively, and stalked out of the room.

Left alone, after Hettie had left to break the news to Albert about the unexpected appearance of his brother Neil, William came to a sudden decision about Sally, and squared his shoulders. "It's no good, I'll have to go and tell her."

He was just bracing himself for the ticklish task when the shop bell tinkled, and in she came. "Ah, Sally darling, I was just on my way to look for you."

"That's funny, so was I," replied Sally, with the light of battle in her eyes. "What's all this about you and Veronica getting together for a cosy supper, so Ma tells me – I thought you promised me you wouldn't see her again?"

William gulped. "Who told you that? I mean, I did and I meant it." Faced with the uphill task of explaining how it all happened – a daunting prospect that was enough to turn the ascent of Mount Everest into an every-day event - he ploughed on doggedly.

"It was all Neil's doing...I mean Aunt Isobel's." He stopped and hurriedly re-phrased his remarks. "He, I mean, she came up with the whole idea."

Sally did a double take, trying to make head or tail of what he was trying to say. Calling the class to order, she rebuked, "Make up your mind, who are we talking about - Neil or Aunt Isobel – and who are they, why we're at it?" While she was speaking, she had the awful feeling she was already beginning to lose her grip on the proceedings.

William wiped his face and started again, back tracking to the beginning. "You see, we – that is, Hettie and I – came to the conclusion that we needed some help – any help we could lay our hands on," he added candidly, "to stop the shop going under. So we phoned Albert's brother, Neil, and asked him. Unfortunately," he started to tread warily, "what we didn't know was that the …um…police were after him." Seeing she was about to ask another tricky question, he went on hurriedly, "It was only some minor offence, and when he turned up, Constable Cuthbert was already here measuring up after the break in, and so Neil decided to disguise himself as a woman, and called himself Aunt Isobel."

Sally's head started spinning as she tried to keep the conversation on a sane level.

"What's that got to do with having supper with Veronica?"

"I was coming to that," replied William hastily, seeing the situation slipping out of hand. "You see, Aunt Isobel, as he was, had this idea of mending fences with Newman."

He looked at Sally triumphantly, as if that explained everything.

At this point, Sally's head started buzzing again. "Mending fences – with Aunt Isobel?"

"No, she, I mean, he was trying to come up with ideas to keep the shop going, otherwise it's all over for Uncle Albert - particularly after Hettie's trouble with Ferdie."

"Ferdie – who's he?"

"She," corrected William distractedly, trying to concentrate. "The cow, of course."

Sally found herself beginning to sag, as she fought desperately against an irresistible desire to giggle, and all her stern resolve began to evaporate.

"The cow... What cow?"

"I'm telling you," answered William feverishly. "Hettie was up all night with Ferdie, her cow, and the vet left some medicine for her on the same day as the doctor who called in with some pills for Albert, after he got injured in that dust-up Hettie had with Mavis."

"What's that got to do with the price of cheese?" gasped Sally in a daze.

"Cheese? – for goodness sake, don't confuse me," said William trying to concentrate. "Don't you see? Newman wandered into Albert's cottage looking for some water to have with his whisky, and took Ferdie's medicine by mistake."

It was too much for Sally. "What did the cow have to do with it?"

William spoke severely, "I'm telling you. He gave Albert's pills to the cow and she felt much better." He paused to consider. "Not like Newman, who got blotto and went to sleep in the pig sty. That's why he wandered in the shop covered in…well, in such a state he frightened the two shop thieves away."

A gust of laughter suddenly engulfed Sally, and washed all her resentment away as she clung to the counter.

"Is that why he turned up looking like the dog's dinner and Veronica was so furious?"

"You've got it. So you see why it's so important to keep them on our side?" urged William.

"Yes, I suppose so," agreed Sally weakly, getting a grip on herself. "But you will promise not to get too friendly with that Veronica again?"

"Of course," promised William devotedly. "I'll make sure we sit poles apart, all evening."

Waiting outside and debating whether to call in and pick up her father's paper, Veronica paused with her hand on the shop door, and caught the tail end of the conversation. "We'll see about that," she said to herself and turned back, all thoughts of the paper forgotten, eager to get her revenge, and already working out ways to go about it.

A few minutes later she burst into her father's study, just as he was sealing up the invitation.

"Paw," she burst out, her fighting blood up in anticipation of the battle ahead. "I've changed my mind. I'll be there – just let them try to stop me."

Chapter Seven
The Get Together

As the supper event drew near, very little could be seen of Hettie, except for sounds of bustling activity from inside her cottage that could be heard up and down the High Street.

However, the term 'bustling' could no way near to describing the agitated state of mind of Albert at that moment. He was wandering around glassy eyed, with the air of a man who has just been slugged by a disgruntled creditor, still trying to take in the shattering thought that a) his wayward brother, who he had fondly believed to be safely ensconced in a far away London suburb, was back in their midst stirring up mayhem, and b) he was on the run from the police, and lastly c) if that wasn't enough, he was going around dressed up as some ghastly pantomime dame.

When Hettie eventually came to look for him, after making a feverish last minute rush to change for the party, she was shocked to see him still in his dressing gown, taking a steady-ing drink from the cocktail cabinet to calm his nerves.

"Albert love, what are you up to," she burst out, nearly making him spill his drink. "D'you realise what the time is? Our guests will be here at any moment."

"Guests, what guests?" he asked vaguely, af-ter taking a sip from another bottle and trying to decide which he preferred on balance.

"Mr Newman and his daughter, Veronica, of course, you silly. William invited them, remem-ber, so we could get to know them better."

"Ah, good lad, William, saved the day with that splendid order of theirs. Remind me to up his salary." He took another experimental sip and approved. "Yes, this one, I think."

"You haven't paid him anything yet," retorted Hettie exasperated. "And if you don't get ready soon, you won't have them much longer as cus-tomers either, while you're still in your dressing gown. You can't expect Neil to take over as host."

Albert choked at the frightful thought. As his memory began to surface, he said plaintively,

"Who asked him to come anyway – dressed up like a dog's dinner?"

Hettie took a deep breath. "William and I did, because we knew you needed some help. So come on, be a love, go and get changed. I'll send William up to help you."

As further strands of memory began to filter through, he cried fretfully, "And why are the police after him, that's what I want to know. What d'you think Newman will think when he finds out?"

Losing her patience, Hettie ticked him off, "I don't know, and we haven't got time to find out. Now are you going to this party, or not? Otherwise I'll have to try to cancel – not that there's much time left to do that now," she added, looking at her watch.

"Oh, all right." He put the bottle down regretfully. "I suppose I'd better." Then to his surprise, he admitted, "I don't know what I'd do without you, Hettie."

Covering up her delight and confusion, Hettie scolded him, "Go on with you, and get dressed, you old silly. Hurry up, I've still got a million and one things to do. I don't know how we're going to get ready in time - the food will all be spoilt, at this rate."

But her forebodings were nothing to the frenzied goings on taking place in the cottage next door. Wails and anguished shrieks could be heard, building up to such a crescendo from Veronica's bedroom that Ed Newman was desperately thinking of calling the whole thing off. First the stockings laddered, then the new dress specially ordered from an expensive boutique off Regent Street developed a tear, and her father was driven to console himself with what remained of the steadily depleting bottle of whisky.

Finally, after completing a hastily arranged repair, Veronica announced she was ready. "Come on, Paw," she commanded critically, taking in the sight of her father sprawled out on the sofa, glass in hand, conveniently overlooking the fact she was largely the cause of the delay. "What have you been doing all this time – we'll be late. How do I look?"

"Fine," he eyed her peevishly, struggling to his feet with an effort. "Let's go then."

Meanwhile, next door, Hettie was trying to instil a welcoming spirit into the gathering before the guests arrived – an exercise that reminded Albert of his father's tales of going over the top in the first World War. And beside him, William was gripped by a nameless fear of what was to come, muttering to himself desperately, "Poles apart, remember, poles apart."

Only Neil seemed to be enjoying himself, coyly twisting a strand of his wig between his fingers, and smiling benevolently all around.

"Albert love, please look as if you're enjoying yourself, and remember to ask Mr Newman how his business is going. If he's feeling really friendly, we might even persuade him to offer William a job if things get worse. And don't forget to be nice to Veronica, William love, we're depending on you."

"Why do I have to wear this blasted stiff collar?" complained Albert, twisting his head to emphasise how uncomfortable he felt. "And do we have to have Neil around – he's bound to give himself away – and then what do we do? Not that we aren't glad to see you, old lad," he added hastily. "It's just the thought of old Cuthbert, that idiot of a bobby, popping his head round the corner, just as we're raising our glasses."

"Don't fret, big bruv, it'll be all right." Neil gave him a brotherly nudge that nearly sent him flying into the drinks trolley. "Just nod me the wink if things get rough, and I'll exert my feminine wiles to smooth things down. You might need my special line of blarney before the night's out," he added jovially, hoisting his bosoms into place.

"Idiot, now look see what you've made me do," complained Albert, bending down stiffly and picking up the bottles off the floor.

"Hush," warned Hettie, "I think they're here, remember what I said. Ah, there you are," she said, raising her voice, "how nice to see you again, Mr Newman. And what a gorgeous dress, Veronica – don't you think so, William?" giving him a meaningful glance.

"How… um…nice." was all William was able to manage before his voice was lost in a polite burst of conversation around him. Seeing Veronica advance purposefully towards him, he hurriedly took refuge in the depths of a well padded sofa in the corner, where he felt reasonably safe, and well out of sight of the gathered throng.

His relief was only temporary however. Before he was able to breathe freely again, a sinuous shape materialised out of thin air, and snuggled up next to him.

"Hello there, handsome," cooed the honey voice of Veronica, pressing up against him, and trapping him in the enveloping depth of the sofa. "I'd almost given up looking for you – where have you been hiding?"

William had that strange feeling that his vocal chords had given up on him, before he finally managed a squawk. "Me?" he stammered. "I thought we weren't in your good books anymore." On second thoughts, he decided not to pursue that line too closely.

"Why, you don't want to take any notice of what I say seriously, honey lamb. Why, that's my old get-up-and-go spirit my Momma taught me. You didn't think I meant it, did you?"

Wishing with all his heart she'd follow her philosophy and get up and go, he caught sight of Hettie making urgent signals at him, and hastened to correct that impression. "No, no, of course not," he assured her hastily, wondering what her next move would be. He was not left in doubt very long. With an athletic leap involving a whir of arms and legs, he found her nestling cosily in his arms.

Blinking with alarm, William cast an agonized look around for signs of help. Instead, all he got was a beaming smile from Hettie who leaned over and whispered, "So nice to see you getting on so well together," and in an aside, "Keep at it, you're doing fine, love."

Just as he was giving up all hope of being rescued, he heard the echoing sounds of a gong resounding, and Neil appeared at the doorway carrying a tray of lifesaving drinks. But he spoilt the effect by nearly tripping over his dress, and had to be rescued by Hettie who rushed to his side to take over.

Much to Veronica's annoyance, and William's profound relief, her father boomed out, "Give a hand, Vee, and help this lovely lady with the drinks."

With a muttered aside, Veronica heaved herself off, and grabbed a couple of glasses for handing out before rushing back to resume her clinch. But William had already made his escape, and stood well away in the middle of a group, with glass raised at the ready.

Noticing his apparent eagerness to join in the toast, Ed Newman leaned over confidentially. "Say, you look like you know something about the good stuff – have you heard where I can get a bottle of something they call, 'Ferdie' around here?"

William started and nearly spilt his drink, and to his horror, Neil looked up innocently nearby, and remarked in a loud voice that made itself heard well above the hum of conversation, "Isn't that the name of that gorgeous old cow of yours, Hettie - the one you were telling me about?"

In the pregnant silence that followed, Hettie tried to laugh it off, and cover up the sudden gagging noise proceeding from Newman. "Goodness, what nonsense you do talk, Aunt Isobel, you're mixing it all up again. She's called 'Purdy', nothing like it. Now you've all had a drink - what about supper?"

In the general murmur of appreciation at the thought of food, the guests were ushered towards the small dining room next door.

During the small talk on the way out, Newman cast an admiring look at Aunt Isobel and murmured, "Gee, anyone tell you you're mighty handsome, m'am?"

"Go on, you naughty man – you say that to all the ladies."

"Only the best, m'am, only the best. May I call you Isobel? Allow me." |He tucked her arm under his elbow. "Now what do you know about this drink they call 'Ferdie'?"

She gave him a playful push that nearly knocked him sideways. "Go on, that's all you men talk about - booze. Now tell me all about your fascinating business – does it really keep us ladies safe in bed at nights?"

With an elaborate wink, he tucked her arm in more firmly, and chuckled, "Not from me, m'am it wouldn't, if I might be so bold to say," remembering in time to move aside, to avoid another hefty shove.

Amid the general flow of conversation that followed around the table Hettie emerged from the kitchen to loud applause, flourishing a large serving plate on which rested a joint of pork, still sizzling from the oven.

"There you are everybody, try this for size," beamed Hettie. "Now who's going to carve?"

As they tucked in, Ed Newman brought up a subject troubling him since they arrived. "Say, what's happened to that cow of yours that kept us awake all night when we got here?"

"Oh, you mean," Hettie nearly called her, 'Ferdie', and stopped herself in time. "She's fit and well again – just a touch of indigestion, that's all."

"Ah, that's something to celebrate then, that's for sure – eh, Vee?"

Still feeling thwarted after her abrupt separation from William, Veronica snorted, "You can say that again, Paw, I thought that damn cow next door would never stop mooing, or sumpting."

"Hah, well this pork is something else again – it's just the tops. Not one of yours, eh Hettie," he enquired jokingly. As she hesitated, he had a sudden vision of an enormous pig peering down at him in the farmyard. Dropping his knife and fork with a clatter, he quavered, "It isn't that big black one, is it?"

"No, of course not," answered Hettie firmly. "It came from another batch altogether. That Blackie is just an old pet – we all love him."

"Gee, thank the Lord," he said reverently. "Say, you can ask me any time, if this is on the menu."

"Funny you should say that," interrupted Neil, lapsing into his normal baritone, before thumping his chest apologetically. "So sorry, indigestion you know." Then pitching his voice higher, he lurched into a falsetto, "Now there's a thing - you were just thinking of starting up a meat counter – weren't you, Hettie?" Then remembering he needed Albert's approval, he trilled, "She's such a treasure, isn't she, Albert – always thinking up new schemes for improving the shop."

Put off by the idea of having a mass of assorted meat spread all over his counter Albert was about to dismiss the idea with a shudder, when Neil kicked him under the table just in time.

"Say," piped up Newman, full of enthusiasm. "That gets my vote for a start. If you do that I'll be in there every day, buying up the shop."

"Oh ah, will you, by George." Albert changed his mind hurriedly at the thought. "Of course, that's exactly what we're planning." His eyes lighting up at the prospect, he enthused, "We'll have the biggest and best meat counter in the County. Put that at the top of our list, Hettie."

"Naturally, we'll have to build it up gradually at first," she cautioned, wondering where she was going to get enough pigs to get the scheme off the ground.

"I'm sure you can manage that," beamed Albert, feeling the promise of new business coursing through his veins. In an attempt to kindle the blossoming friendship with his new neighbour, he remembered to enquire with some warmth, "And how is your business coming along over here, Newman – satisfactorily, I hope?"

"Only so-so, so far," admitted his guest. "I came over here to ginger up the business, as you may have heard." He drummed his fingers on the table. "Like you, I need new clients to build it up – and I need to bring on a new team of specialists to handle the accounts – very difficult these days. They either know too much and want to move on, or they know nuttin, and we can't spare the staff to train them."

He felt in his pocket for his cigar case and getting permission to go ahead, started chewing the butt end meditatively for a moment, before lighting up and drawing on it contentedly.

"I don't mind telling you between friends," glancing around for confirmation before going on, "that I've got a mighty fine security contract brewing with one of your local people right here in town, but I'm a bit thin on ground regarding staff – say, you don't know of any suitable qualified candidates knocking around?"

Hettie gave a delicate cough, and catching Albert's eye, nodded meaningly at William.

Albert hesitated, and tried to get his nephew's attention with a notable lack of success. Aware he was becoming the centre of attention, William shifted uneasily in his chair and looked studiously at the floor, pretending to count the patterns on the carpet.

Clearing his throat after further prompts from Hettie, Albert waved a hand at William. "If you're looking for a bright young lad who's keen to carve out a career for himself, you could do no better than consider my nephew here. At the moment, he is filling in his spare time giving us his valuable advice on…"

"Marketing strategy," prompted Neil encouragingly.

"Exactly." Albert shot him a grateful glance. "As you know, marketing strategy is vitally important in all branches of business, and I'm sure you would find him a keen learner."

"Gee whizz," came endorsement closer to home. "I think that's a brilliant idea, Paw – he's certainly a fast worker, am I telling you."

"Hem…quite so," concurred Albert, tactfully. "I can vouch for the fact that he is a hard worker, and well deserves recognition for his achievements to date."

"Is that so," mused Newman, twirling his cigar reflectively. "What experience have you had so far, young man?"

Before William could answer, Hettie contributed brightly, "He has already made quite a name for himself locally in the newspaper world," a well intentioned remark that had William squirming with embarrassment, after his recent experiences as a reporter. At the same time, he was gripped with dawning horror at the prospect of getting involved in anything that would mean closer contact with Veronica.

In the hope of killing the idea stone dead, he protested loudly, "I got the push, if that's what you mean."

Hettie had a sudden fit of coughing, and Aunt Isobel broke in smoothly, "Not literally, of course. He's so modest. William was encouraged to leave, to take on more ambitious projects, that's what you meant, wasn't it, my dear?"

"Well, you good people, I will certainly think it over," promised Newman, getting to his feet regretfully. "And now we must leave you, after a most enjoyable meal."

"But you can't go yet," insisted Neil, cooing, "Can they, Albert?" giving his brother a nudge. "We haven't passed the port around yet, and haven't you got something special lurking in the cellar, Albert, to round off the evening?"

After a pause, Albert rose to the occasion with a painful smile, hiding the anguish of a connoisseur about to lose the cream of his collection he'd put by for a special occasion. "Of course, I was forgetting, if you'll excuse me a moment – you will be able to stay on for that, I trust," he faltered, hoping for a reprieve.

"Gee, if you put it like that, how can I refuse?" beamed Newman, settling back more comfortably in his seat.

After seeing his best port being passed around the table for the umpteenth time, Albert settled back with a resigned sigh, thinking nothing else was likely to happen to ruin his evening that could possibly compete with the loss of some of his favourite wine collection.

William for his part was beginning to relax his guard with the increased signs of convivial banter, and the reassuring fact that he was seated well out of reach from Veronica, on the opposite side of the table – but they were both wrong.

Seeing she was no longer the centre of attention, Veronica jumped up from the table with an enthusiastic whoop. "Gee, I know what – what about some charades?" Before anyone could object she grabbed hold of the holdall she'd left by the door and disappeared into the kitchen with a wave of the hand.

"Well, I guess we'd better shift ourselves to the sitting room, with your permission, Albert," said Newman getting to his feet with difficulty. "Kinda cramped for those sort of games in here."

"Of course, of course. Er, what are we likely to expect – nothing too drawn out, I trust, Newman?" Albert asked anxiously, looking at the clock.

"Call me 'Ed'," begged his guest earnestly. "After that fabulous meal, you're my friend for life." Gazing owlishly after his daughter, he added, "Say, anything could happen with that whacky kid of mine. I've given up trying to guess - after you, old buddy."

Contrary to Albert's concern, they didn't have to wait long. Within a few minutes, the door sprang open and with a loud 'huzzah!' and Veronica pirouetted into the room wearing a flimsy dress that left little to the imagination.

William instinctively closed his eyes at the revealing sight, and in doing so had no time to take evasive action before Veronica launched herself onto his lap again.

"Here, Paw, get a load of this," she cried, tossing him her mobile. "Put it in the family album. This is for keeps," and with that she turned and flung her arms around William and planted a smacking great kiss on his lips, with plenty of follow through. "How about that, lover boy?"

"Poles apart," was all William was able to mumble. "Poles apart."

Chapter Eight
Up Against It

Anxious to hear how the party went, Sally called in at the village shop on her way to school the next morning. Inside, she found William in the midst of a furious activity, whilst nervously praying news of the previous night's revelry had not leaked out while he helped Neil to shift units around to make up the new meat counter. In case anyone might be left in doubt, a large banner adorned the wall behind emblazoned with the slogan, 'Buy your fresh farm meat here'.

Casting an anxious eye over the scene, Albert leaned on his stick, shaking his head doubtfully.

"Are you sure this is going to work, Neil?"

His brother massaged his shoulder reassuringly. "Of course, it will, big bruv. They'll be rolling up in their droves before you know what's hit you. We'll be rivalling Fortnum and Mason at this rate, you'll see."

Still not convinced, Albert turned to Hettie anxiously. "What d'you think, Het? Will we get our supplies on time?"

"Don't fuss, Albert, everything's fine," Hettie said automatically, taking a peep at her watch for the umpteenth time, and darting to the door again to see if there was any sign of the delivery van.

"Quick, here he is – give us a hand, love," she cried suddenly at William, as the door swung open and a truck appeared, laden with meat products, and backing up to the shop.

"What's going on?" Sally called out, as William hurried past to help.

"Can't stop – we're opening up any minute, and there's nothing on the counter."

"How did the party go?"

At the mention of the party, William started guiltily and nearly dropped a load. "Er, fine – we're setting up as a farm shop – it's all Neil's idea. Mr Newman has promised to put in a big order, and we're expecting him any minute to give him first choice," he explained hastily. "That sounds like him now, must dash."

"I'm so glad," but her good wishes had fallen on deaf ears. William was already bounding to the door, ready to usher in their favoured customer to set the ball rolling, leaving Sally feeling flat and strangely alone.

Her unhappiness was intensified as the door open, and in swept Veronica followed by a reporter and photographer, hot on her heels from the local paper.

"Pa and I are so thrilled to be the first ones to help this new enterprise get on the road," she gushed, placing her hand possessively on William's arm. "With the help of my good friend, William Bridge here – my *very* good friend," she emphasised, flashing a smile of triumph at Sally, as she passed.

The reporter perked up and looked hopefully at the highly embarrassed William, who by now was wishing the ground would swallow him up.

"Any announcement due on that front, Miss Veronica?"

Veronica looked coy. "Well, all I can tell you is we sure had a swell party last night to celebrate the opening, and things are looking good and we hope to make an announcement real soon.

Meantime, let's just say I've promised your sub-editor some interesting pictures – like this one." With that she flipped open her mobile and gave the reporter a tantalising glimpse, before holding it up over their heads to make sure Sally had a good look, showing her sitting on William's lap with her arms around his neck.

There was a quick gasp from Sally and she turned to leave, trying to hide a numbing shock that left her seething.

"Wait, Sally," protested William tearing himself away. "It wasn't like that."

But the damage was done, and Sally slammed out of the shop, blinded by tears, vowing she would have nothing more to do with him.

Veronica tucked her mobile away, well satisfied with her performance.

After the opening as the crowds drifted away, William put in an urgent call to his friend, Malcolm, on the Globe.

Although delighted at the opportunity to give his old friend a plug, Malcolm could make no sense about his reluctance to back up Veronica's announcement.

"What d'you mean, you don't want it mentioned, mate – she sounds a real honey…oh, like that, is it? Well…" he sounded doubtful. "I don't know if I can do anything about killing a direct quote, but I'll tell you what, we could manage to lose the pic - but what can we put in its place? I know," he bellowed, inspired by a sudden thought that made William cringe at the memory – "what about that whacky sketch of yours?"

"No, leave it to me," he said, brushing aside William's agonised protests. "See you, mate, must go – give us a ring sometime," and the line went dead, leaving William staring numbly at the receiver.

William recalled the look of rage on the sub-editor's face at the sight of the sketch, and shuddered at what he might do. But his predicament paled against the immediate problem of how to put things right with Sally.

Casting a quick look round and satisfied his presence would not be noticed in the crush, he slipped away and decided to have it out with Sally face to face before it was too late.

Drawing a blank at the station taxi rank, he set out resolutely to walk the five miles to the

Castle, where he hoped to intercept Sally during the lunch break.

Sally was so noticeably upset while taking her lessons that morning, that when the news filtered back to the Head during morning break, he was relieved to hear there was a phone message from her stepmother, Lady Courtney, urgently requesting her to return home immediately.

It was an unusually subdued Sally who returned home that lunch hour, feeling battered and crushed by her shattering experience at the shop, to be greeted by her mother, triumphantly flourishing a copy of the local paper in her face.

"What do you call this then?" she accused, not attempting to conceal a look of 'I told you so' in her face.

"Oh that," accepted Sally wearily, trying to appear indifferent. "I know all about that – the village shop is opening up a new meat and poultry line."

"I am not referring to that," replied her mother icily, "it's the story underneath about that William character you're so attached to that's caught everyone's notice – the one, in case you have conveniently forgotten, who's been playing fast and loose with that poor girl of Ed-ward's yet again. Oh, the shame of it. It says here they are hoping to get married! How could you allow yourself to be taken in – it's quite obvious he's after her father's money."

"That's not true, let me see," protested Sally, trying unsuccessfully to thrust all thoughts of the unpleasant accusation from her mind. But even as she spoke, her trusting nature was receiving a severe battering. She scanned the paper, and was relieved to see the picture Veronica had taken on her mobile was not included – instead there was a cartoon depicting various Town Hall notables dressed up as farmyard animals, and someone with his arms wrapped around the Town Clerk.

Overcoming a momentary giggle at the sight, she could not ignore the message Veronica's words implied. After his latest behaviour, she was beginning to wonder how she had been idiot enough to believe she had ever been in love with him.

"Anyway, enough is enough." Her mother dismissed her protestations with an imperious wave of her hand. "Your father and I have decided it's time you settled down and got married to a good man of some standing in whom we have the utmost trust, who will look after you, and see you don't get involved in any more of these disgusting episodes that are making us a laughing stock of the County – isn't that right, Henry?"

Sir Henry looked uncomfortable. "Well, he does seem to be making a bit of a hash of things, doesn't he love?" racking his brains to say something in the lad's defence.

"He certainly needs a talking to," agreed Sally wanly.

"I don't blame you entirely, Sally my dear," her mother unbent graciously, seeing how crushed Sally seemed. "We all made mistakes when we were young, didn't we Henry?"

His mouth opened and closed, as his wife swept on without waiting for a reply.

"I remember being pursued by all kinds of young men who were falling over themselves to take me out, but something told me to wait for the right man, and then your father came along and refused to take 'no' for an answer, didn't you Henry?"

Ignoring the wistful look that flitted over Sir Henry's face, she allowed herself a sentimental sigh. "We've never regretted it, have we, Henry?" She turned majestically to Sally. "You see, we're thinking of your future, my dear. Don't forget, you won't always have us here to look after you. And so we have decided you really must settle down and give up all those silly ideas of getting entangled with that unsuitable young man."

Forestalling Sally's half-hearted protest, she went on, "Now I know you and Clive got off on the wrong foot, but I – we do feel you should give it another go, so we have asked Clive to come here this afternoon to apologise for his rather...over enthusiastic behaviour, and see if we can start all over again. You will do this to please us, won't you, Sally?"

Seeing her father studiously studying at his shoes, as if inspecting them closely before being called out on parade, Sally sighed, giving up hope of any support from that quarter, and found herself meekly agreeing.

"Good," her mother nodded as if that settled the matter. "Right," she checked her watch as the doorbell pealed. "Good, that must be him now. Come in."

It was a completely different Clive who presented himself. Gone was that blatantly arrogant self-satisfied approach he had adopted the last time they met. In its place was a seemingly humble and contrite young man who was anxious to re-establish himself in her good books.

"How good of you to see me," he murmured deferentially. "After my awful bad manners last time, I was afraid you'd never want to see me again."

Remembering their last encounter, Sally was on the point of retorting but found herself relapsing back into an unaccustomed submissive mood, merely making polite conversation.

Relieved, Clive took her hand and while devoutly assuring her of his respectful attentions, asked her almost pleadingly if there was any remote chance she might possibly reconsider his proposal.

As her parents waited with bated breath, to her mother's delighted astonishment and to her father's disappointment, she found herself accepting.

"My dear, how wonderful," breathed Lady Courtney, wreathed in smiles. "We must put an announcement in the papers immediately, mustn't we, Henry, and we'll have a little party to celebrate - just one or two close friends. What about your family, Clive, would they like to join us – how about your father?"

"No, I'm afraid he's not free at the moment – affairs of State, you know," said Clive hastily, omitting to mention that his father, known to his intimates as 'Soapy' Joe, on account of his ability as a safecracker, was detained on that and other pressing matters at Her Majesty's pleasure.

"Your mother, perhaps?" pressed Lady Courtney, not to be outdone.

"I'm afraid she's awfully busy as well just now - organising a 'coming out' party in the West Country, I'm afraid." He could have added she was unsuccessfully trying to organise a break-out at Dartmoor where her husband was being held, but prudently thought it best not to elaborate.

His hesitation served to fuel Sir Henry's suspicions about the young man that had taken root from the moment they were first introduced, and as soon as the party broke up he made his excuses and retired to his study to put in a call to his solicitor, Andrew Partridge, and poured out his misgivings. Satisfied with his friend's promise to look into the matter, he decided to search out Sally and have a heart to heart talk about it.

Catching sight of her in the conservatory, he plumped himself down in a chair next to her and squeezed her hand. "Care to tell me about it, Sal?"

Looking up with tear-streaked face, Sally appealed, "I seem to have made a bit of a mess of things, haven't I?"

"Nonsense," he consoled gently. "We all make mistakes when we're young – even your stepmother admits it." They both giggled at the thought.

"Look." He hesitated. "I'm not much of an expert on the subject these days, particularly since your dear mother passed away, but look here. Why don't you go and have a word with young William about it. There may be a perfectly rational explanation for it all and he struck me as quite a likeable young man."

Having arrived hot and tired at the tail end of the conversation after unsuccessfully scouring the grounds in search of Sally, the young man in question heard the last remark and beamed gratefully at Sir Henry.

"Thank heavens someone is willing to believe me – what about you, Sally? Please say you do," he begged.

"I thought you said, 'poles apart'?" replied Sally coldly. "You promised you wouldn't go anywhere near her."

"But I didn't," protested William vehemently. "I give you my word – it was all her doing." Seeing her waver, he insisted, "All the others were ganging up on me because they were afraid of losing Newman's orders." Throwing caution to the winds, he went down on one knee, "I couldn't let Uncle down, he was nearly giving up – it would have been the end of his dream."

"I know, that's why I trusted you." Sally sat there wrestling with her feelings, not knowing what to believe. "Why should I trust you now?"

"Because I love you," he said simply. "I think I fell in love with you the moment you walked into our shop."

"Did you really?" Sally found herself weakening, and tentatively traced a line over his face, letting him kiss her fingers.

"Hem," her father coughed tactfully in the background. "Aren't we forgetting one thing – Clive for instance?"

"Oh, no!" Sally jumped up with her hand to her mouth. "You're going to hate me for this," she said miserably. "I was so wretched after seeing that story, I let myself say 'Yes' to Clive. Oh, darling, will you ever forgive me?"

"Of course," swallowed William, taken aback. Pulling himself together, he promised fervently, "He won't get the chance – not while I'm around."

Making a dramatic entrance, Lady Courtney appeared at the doorway and fixed William with an imperious gaze that would have shrivelled any lesser man on the spot, but William stood his ground.

"Henry! What is Mr Bridge doing here?"

Seeing her father hesitate, Sally stepped forward in front of William like a lioness protecting her young. "Ma," she announced determinedly, "I am not going to marry Clive – I'm going to marry William, and nothing you can say is going to stop me!"

"We'll see about that," snapped Lady Courtney. "Henry, do something."

A faint tinkling bell sounded in the distance, and Sir Henry sprang into life. "That's the phone," he mumbled. "Call I was waiting for, must dash," and disappeared into his study.

"Very well," thundered her stepmother, and pressed a bell.

In seconds, a footman materialised at a run, well used to her summons.

"Jason, show Mr Bridge out," she commanded.

"Yes, m'lady. This way, sir."

Accustomed to her stepmother's moods, Sally turned to William with a look of sudden determination. "Don't worry about me, darling - you go. I'll see to this."

Not wishing to cause a scene, William gave Sally a reassuring look, and murmured, "Don't let the old dragon get you down – I'll be back," and reluctantly allowed himself to be led out, leaving Sally to face the full wrath of her stepmother.

"Right, now I have your attention, young lady," she sniffed, dismissing Sally's protests as of no account, as if they had merely surfaced in a temporary moment of insanity, "I would draw your attention to the fact that your fiancé, Clive, is waiting in the hall and wishes to see you." She gave a grotesque smile of encouragement that ended up somewhere between a scowl and a simper. "I gather he wishes to make a small presentation as a token of his admiration." She flourished her lorgnette as a signal of her displeasure. "I trust you will say nothing that will diminish our regard for Clive." And pressing a bell and giving her instructions to admit their guest, she remained where she was to ensure her wishes were carried out to the letter.

Ushered in by the footman, Clive bounded forward with an ingratiating smile.

"Ah, there you Sally, I thought you might like to wear this little something I picked up at the jewellers this morning," omitting to mention that the jeweller in question was looking the other way at the time, "until I can get you a proper engagement ring," he added hurriedly, noticing her complete lack of interest.

His announcement was interrupted by the return of Sir Henry exhibiting an almost jaunty side of his nature, following his illuminating phone call.

"Ah, there you are, Henry," observed Lady Courtney somewhat acidly. "I'm glad you can spare the time. Come and see what Clive has bought for Sally."

"Capital, capital," beamed Sir Henry, examining the stone closely. "My goodness, that must have set you back a tidy sum, young man."

"Henry!" his wife was scandalised. "I'm sure dear Clive is not worried about the cost of an engagement ring!"

"Well, he'll need to, if he's going to make some sense out of our almighty overheads," remarked Sir Henry breezily. Pausing to ensure his remarks had sunk in, he added casually, "There can't be many estates as broke as we are."

"Henry!"

Lady Courtney's wail broke the scandalised silence.

Clive's face, though not normally a healthy tan, took on a greenish pallor that in any other less nourished individual might have indicated an imminent demise.

"Broke?" he managed feebly. Then galvanised by an instinctive measure of self-preservation, he clutched at his chest theatrically, "My heart!" He staggered to the door, making profuse apologies. "Excuse me, Lady Courtney, I get these attacks from time to time – I must see my doctor." In passing, he grabbed at the box containing the ring, and slipping it in his pocket vanished from sight, leaving the air vibrating with unspoken accusations.

"Henry! How could you, now look what you've done."

"Yes, I fancy I've put the kybosh on his nasty little scheme," remarked Sir Henry placidly.

Lady C clutched at her heart dramatically. "After all the trouble I've taken to cultivate Clive, you go and do this to me."

"You might be interested to know," said Sir Henry buoyantly, ignoring her agonised protests, "that the call I've just had from Andrew Partridge, our solicitor, has confirmed everything I suspected, ever since I first set eyes on that young rogue."

"What was that?" begged Sally, overjoyed at the unexpected turn of events.

"Only that this worthless individual, who you have been royally entertaining, who goes by the name of Clive Brand, amongst other numerous aliases, is nothing but a conman!" Sir Henry announced cheerfully, beginning to enjoy himself. "Apparently, he is well known for worming his way into unsuspecting households, and relieving them of their valuables, and any loose cash he can get his hands on."

"Oh Henry!" came renewed wails from Lady Courtney, as she slid down off the end of the settee with a crash.

Chapter Nine
Lady C Hits Back

Lying prostrate on her bed, with an ice pack applied to her forehead to help calm her feverish nerves, Lady Courtney stared listlessly up at the ceiling trying to draw inspiration from the faded pattern above her head, in the vain hope it would somehow provide a much needed clue to help extricate herself from the present impossible situation. Dismissing the timely rescue her husband had achieved as a personal slight on her own judgement, she concentrated all her attention on thinking up ways of getting rid of William once and for all as a prospective son-in-law. She squeezed the ice pack with renewed vigour to help her think, spurred on by the dreadful prospect of having a local tradesman of all people foisted on them, and joining the imposing line of family portraits in the long gallery – an appalling fate too hideous to contemplate.

She was interrupted by a knock at the door, and the timorous face of Mary, her maid, peered around the corner to see what sort of mood she was in.

"Beg your pardon, m'am, there's a gentleman asking to see someone."

"Not now," came the wearied response. Then curiosity overcame her. "Who is it?"

"He said his name was Foxey, m'am."

Lady Courtney knitted her brows in an effort to think where she had heard the name before. Foxey, Foxey, why did it sound so familiar? Then illumination hit her. Of course - Mavis Foxey's husband.

Interrupting her train of thoughts, the maid asked helpfully, "Shall I ask Sir Henry to see him?"

"On no account should he be disturbed," she said hastily. Knowing her husband was safely shut away in his study wrestling with the estate accounts, she thought swiftly. "Show the gentle-man into the…summer house, Mary. And bring some tea there when I call."

"Yes, m'am."

A few minutes later after repairing her make-up, she was striding into the summerhouse graciously holding out a hand. "Mr. Foxey, I've heard so much about you – how can I help you?"

Overhearing the visitor's name being announced, Sally stopped in her tracks outside on the way to her room, and after a thoughtful glance, changed direction and tip-toed up to the door to listen in with increasing interest.

* * *

Meanwhile, back in the village shop, to take his mind off his immediate problems William was plunged into the task of helping to deal with the flood of shoppers attracted by the sight of the new meat counter and all it contained. In short, the shop was doing a roaring trade, watched over benevolently by Neil, who kept a low profile in the background.

When the call eventually came through from Sally the demands for service had become so frantic William had great difficulty in finding someone to relieve him at the counter.

"Tell her I'll ring back," he called out hopefully.

"She says it's urgent."

"Right then. Hang on to this a second."

169

Before he had a chance to refuse Neil found himself being handed an apron by his nephew, who disappeared into the office and was immediately engaged in an animated conversation.

All Neil could hear was a whoop of 'what?' and 'you don't mean it?', and the rest of the conversation was lost as Neil was distracted by a beery face appearing in front of him demanding, "And I'll have two of those plump ones, luv."

"You saucy beast," was his automatic response, before his attention was drawn to a row of chickens laid out in a row before him.

Inside the office, William listened with growing appreciation at the latest news.

"So thanks to Dad I'm free from that awful Clive at last!" cried Sally. "Isn't that great?"

"You mean to say he's nothing but a fraud?" repeated William bewildered. "But how did he manage to take your stepmother in?"

"Because she believed what she wanted to, I suppose."

"Does that mean there's nothing to stop us getting married?" exclaimed William joyfully.

There was a pause, and the voice at the other end took on a more cautious note.

"That was the good news." Sally's voice sounded serious all of a sudden. "Now for the not-so-good. You'll never guess. Ma had a visitor just afterwards who turned out to be a Mr Foxey - I think he's the husband of that Mavis who was up to no good in the shop with your Uncle Albert."

"What did he want?"

Sally hesitated at the other end. "I'm not sure. He started off by sounding Ma out about some grandiose plan he had for putting the village on the map to attract more tourists, and just as it got to the interesting bit they went into a huddle and I couldn't hear any more."

"Hm," William pondered. "Have you spoken to your dad about it? Perhaps he knows something."

"No, poor dear, he's been stuck in his study all morning trying to make head or tail of the estate accounts."

"Well, find an excuse and get him on his own and ask him – he's the only one who might know."

Sally sounded doubtful. "I'll try, but Ma can be very secretive when she wants – she may not have told him. Shuts up like a clam sometimes, then wham, she hits you for six when you least expect it."

"I can well imagine," said William with feeling, remembering his last encounter. "Anyway, do your best – he's our only hope. Don't let her get you down."

"I will," Sally promised. "Do you still love me?"

"Of course I do," was his devoted response.

Cheered up, Sally blurted out, "Me too, tons and tons. Help, must dash, someone's coming – speak to you later when I get some news," and rang off.

William stood staring at the telephone still blissfully absorbed by the exchange. Then as he reluctantly turned back to the counter he couldn't help experiencing a passing feeling of unease at Sally's report.

As soon as he had an opportunity, he voiced his misgivings to Neil, who only half listened as he kept one eye on the queue forming outside.

"Looks as if the old girl is itching to get her own back – fill me in on this Foxey character. Make it snappy, I've got to get back."

William obediently went over the background again, describing briefly Mavis Foxey's attempts to use the threat of scandal to turn the locals against the village shop, and how Ted, who did some work for the builder, had recently warned him not to trust Foxy Fred, as he was known.

"Hm." Neil stroked his chin, making a passing mental note that he needed a shave. "I wonder what he's up to? Look, I haven't time to find out just now, what with getting this shop off the ground and everything - I'll have to ask you to do some scouting for me." He cocked a speculative eye at William, "Can I rely on you to do that, my son?"

"Of course," agreed William. "Leave it to me. Knowing Foxey," he added darkly, "he's likely to get up to anything."

They didn't have to wait long. Next morning the first signs appeared that signalled all was not well. First, one of Hettie's prize pigs went off her food, then things began to happen to the regular meat deliveries. One of the lorries suffered a broken axle, then the back-up truck went missing and the driver was found half drunk in a nearby field. At first they put it down to bad luck, but the driver insisted his drink had been spiked, and when the broken axle was inspected there were suspicious signs of tampering. As the rumours started flying around, the locals began to melt away, and started visiting the supermarket down in the town.

"It's only a temporary blip," insisted Neil doing his best to keep the spirit up as Albert showed signs of nervousness. "What's happening at your end?" he asked his nephew in an aside.

"Still trying," William reported exasperated. "They keep telling me Sally's out."

He thought for a moment. "I know," he exclaimed, with a flash of inspiration. "I'll ask Ted. If it's anything to do with Foxey, Ted would know – he's in the building line himself."

"Can you trust him?" asked Neil doubtfully. "If he's worked for Foxey anything he says might be a bit dodgy, if you know what I mean."

"No," said William shaking his head. "Ted's a good sort. He's warned me against Foxey before. He'll be in later for his usual baccy - I'll see if he knows anything."

But Ted was equally puzzled and bristled when William tackled him on the subject. "What do you mean - in the same line of business?" he demanded indignantly. "Are you trying to give our trade a bad name? He's your Mr Fixit – first in the queue if there's a chance of big money around the corner. All I know is he seems pleased as punch with himself these days. If you ask me, I think he's got designs on your place. He rubs his hands every time he sees it." Ted looked around the shop speculatively, as he rolled his cigarette, "If I were you, Chief, I'd check up on things. He may be planning a takeover bid - knowing old Foxey."

His remarks started another train of thought in William. "If that's his game, d'you think he might be behind all these delivery hold-ups?"

"Could be, could be. It makes sense, don't it? If the shop gets a bad name and sales fall off, he'd get it at a knock down price, stands to reason," argued Ted.

"Thanks," said William thoughtfully. "This needs thinking about."

"Anytime, Squire. See you."

It was a pensive William who reported back to Neil.

"Why the cheeky beggar." Neil turned the news over in his mind. "I think this calls for a confab with big bruv, Bertie. Care to come along?"

"I'm right behind you," promised William.

"Well I'll be blowed," was all Albert could think of saying when they tackled him.

He digested William's information, but was just as baffled as Ted had been.

"I've no idea who owns the lease," he admitted after William put the question. "All I know is I answered an advert in the papers about the shop, put there by the local estate agents. They never did tell me who they were acting for."

"But didn't you ask them?" Neil asked incredulously.

"I was only too pleased to get hold of it," said Albert simply. "I'd always got my eye on the shop after coming across it on a coach outing, and when the opportunity came up I grabbed at it with both hands."

"And what were the terms of the lease?" said William, his news sense homing in on the essentials.

"I don't actually own a lease," confessed his uncle. "I just pay a monthly rent to the estate agents."

"What?" Neil looked at his brother in amazement. "But...but what sort of protection have you got?"

"I think Uncle means what kind of arrangement do you have for running it?" put in William more tactfully. "How much notice do you have to give if you wanted to leave, for instance?"

"Why, I believe it is something like six months on either side." Albert tried to remember. "My accountant might know...oh, but I think he's away at the moment."

Neil uttered a strangled comment that expressed his pent up feelings.

"What we need to find out is, who owns the lease?" voiced William thoughtfully. "Until we know that we're running around in circles."

"What about your paper?" Neil turned to his nephew hopefully. "They're good at finding out things like that."

William had an instant vision of his former sub-editor and shuddered. "I don't know about that. I might get one of my mates there to dig up something, though."

"You do that," encouraged Neil. "Meanwhile, we've got a business to run, eh Bertie?"

Albert came out of a mental fog. "Yes, of course. Quite right, there's a thousand things to do. I must phone up our suppliers and find out what's happened to those pies they promised."

"Yes, you do that," said Neil as he patted William on the back. "Meanwhile lad, get on to your chums right away, and get us that info pronto – we're relying on you, lad."

Keen as he was, William should have known it was not the right time to ask, as soon as he got through to his old friend, Malcolm.

"Not now, mate, we're just going to press. I'll ring you back," was the terse response.

Half an hour later he rang back, as good as his word. "Now then, what's it all about?"

"The village shop?" William could almost hear him scratching his head. "The easy ones first, eh? Hang on, that rings a bell. Give me a minute. That's right. We ran a feature on the village a while back, I seem to remember – before your time. I remember digging out background stuff on the history of some of the buildings. As soon as things die down I'll rustle up something. Mind you I'll have to be a bit careful – after slipping in that sketch of yours, I thought we'd never hear the last of it." He chuckled. "But it was worth it, just to see his face. Ta."

When he did come back, his answer brought a heartfelt feeling of relief to William, and he couldn't wait to tell the others.

"It's all right," he assured Neil. "As far as Malcolm can find out, according to the original lease, the rent gets passed on to Sir Henry, Sally's dad. They've been doing it that way since he started the village shop."

But his reply left Neil puzzled. "Then why is this Foxey guy so confident about taking over, and why did he go to see Lady C?"

William scratched his head. "Search me. The only way we'll find out is to ask the agents."

Neil pondered. "How are we going to do that? It might take weeks."

"Okay, I'll phone Sally and get her to sound out her dad – the sooner we find out the better."

"Good man – I knew we could rely on you."

William was as good as his word. A quick call to Sally found her eager to help, and intrigued to find the answer. Less than half an hour later she turned up, wanting to hear all about it.

"Sir Henry, is he um…?" began Neil tactfully.

Divining the thought in his mind, Sally had no hesitation in reassuring him. "He's a baa lamb. You could ask him anything." Then she added cautiously, "As long as it doesn't mean going against my stepmother's wishes."

"But do you think he'd be able to help us… um…sort this 'ere mess out?" Neil stumbled over the best way to put it.

"What he means is, why don't we ask him to come over and find out what Lady C's been up to?" asked William simply, putting into words what they had all been thinking.

"Exactly, couldn't put it better myself." Neil breathed a sigh of relief. "Can you swing it, luv?"

"Wait a minute," interjected Hettie anxiously. "It isn't going to upset relations with Mr Newman next door? I mean, Lady Courtney is an old friend of his, I understand, and we wouldn't want to cause any unpleasantness. It sounds as if we might be prying into her Ladyship's affairs."

"Good thinking, Hettie," backed up Albert automatically, not quite sure where the discussion was heading.

"But Hettie," admonished Neil virtuously, "we're expanding our circle of contacts – it's normal business practice."

"Sir Henry would naturally like to see where Sally helps out in her spare time, and be satisfied about her working conditions," William suggested helpfully.

"And if I ask him, I know he'd only be too pleased to help – you wouldn't need to be involved in any way," said Sally, settling the argument.

"Oh, that's all right then." Hettie gave in reluctantly.

"Good, that settles it," beamed Neil. "When can you fix it?"

William could have told him that with Sally teacher's training behind her, the meeting was as good as arranged. Not that her father needed any encouragement. He had a soft spot for Sally and anything he could do to push it along was okay by him. After his minor triumph in exposing Clive, he was only too keen to roll up his sleeves and do all in his powers to help, even if it was from the sidelines – bearing in mind his wife's formidable stand on the matter.

So it was that they were all assembled the following evening after shop hours, when the blinds could be pulled down in case of word getting out about the meeting.

In deference to his position as manager, Albert was asked to chair the proceedings which he did so after much clearing of the throat.

"So glad you were able to come, Sir Henry," he began. "It was very good of you to attend our little gathering."

"Only too pleased to help." Sir Henry looked around affably. "I hear the shop's doing splendidly at last, all due to your efforts. Glad to hear it."

Seizing on his remark, Albert bent forward eagerly. "Quite so. It's about the shop that we asked you here today, Sir Henry. It has come to our attention, or rather, we were anxious to know if you…ah, I mean, whether you may be…" He started to flounder.

Seeing his uncle falter, William decided to take a hand. "What Uncle is trying to find out is whether you have sold the shop to that man, Foxey, across the road?"

"Good heavens no!" said Sir Henry astonished. "Why on earth would I do an idiotic thing like that? He's the last person I would have any dealings with. Feller's a menace – had the infernal impudence to ask if we could do a crafty deal about putting up some wretched touristy shacks on our estate. Imagine it!"

There was a noticeable release of tension all round at his answer.

Albert beamed at William for getting down to the nub of the problem so speedily, and saving him the embarrassment of asking. "You don't know what a tremendous load you've taken off my mind, Sir Henry. I am most grateful."

"Nonsense, my dear fellow. Only too happy to oblige."

"But in that case," said Sally, struck by a sudden thought, "why was Ma so pally with him yesterday when he came to see us?"

Sir Henry became more guarded. "Nothing to do with me, my love. I have enough trouble getting rid of all those dreadful young men she's always trying to foist on us." He turned to tell the others about the latest one, with a hint of triumph. "Like that Clive Brand fellow, or Smith or whatever his name is. Turned out to be an imposter, didn't he."

"You were marvellous, Dad," enthused Sally. "He soon disappeared when you told him about the state of our finances. He thought we were loaded."

Sir Henry snorted. "You'd think she'd be happy with all those rents we get coming in, instead of trying to snare some deluded well heeled idiot into investing in the estate."

William, who had been gazing fatuously at Sally as they were speaking was brought back to earth by an agonised gurgle from Albert as the remark sank home, and a sharp dig in the ribs from Neil.

"What rents?" his uncle mouthed.

Stirred into action, William put the question. "What rents would those be?"

There was a sharp intake of breath, as everyone leaned forward waiting for his reply.

Sir Henry looked up, mildly surprised. "Eh, oh various odds and ends of property rents I passed over to Margery, to pay off her dress bills when we got married, don't you know."

"Mostly farm rents, I suppose, Pa," encouraged Sally, as if talking to a wayward child.

"Oh, no, nothing like that. I needed those to pay for the upkeep of the bally estate. No, little odds and ends from some of the small town properties. Things like that."

William tried laughing off the remark jokingly. "Not the village shop, I hope?"

"Good heavens, no." Sir Henry was horrified at the suggestion. "The agents would have told me, if that was the case. No, you can rest assured that the village shop is safe."

"Oh, splendid news," exclaimed Albert, mopping his face. "I knew we could rely on you, Sir Henry."

"Wait a minute," reminded Sally, as the thought niggled at the back of her mind. "Why should Ma spend her time hob-knobbing with that man Foxey, if that was the case?"

"Oh, it could be any manner of reasons," said Sir Henry indulgently. "It could be she's looking for some way of getting her own back. I mean, I did rather spike her plans with that young rogue, Clive, if you remember."

"Good, that's settled," beamed Albert. "Now we can get back to running the business again."

"And I can go and see to my animals," agreed Hettie, satisfied.

"All the same," persisted William, remembering Lady C's hostility to their matrimonial plans, as well as opposing everything connected with the running of the shop, "it wouldn't do any harm to check with the estate agents, just to make sure?"

"Good thinking, young William," approved Neil, as Sir Henry began to demur.

"I don't know, do you think that's absolutely necessary?" he questioned uncertainly.

Albert maintained a tactful silence, although it was obvious from his expression where his vote lay.

Seeing him waver, Sally saw it was up to her to steel her father to the task. "Go on, Pa – you'll always be wondering what she's up to, if you don't find out."

"I'm sure your solicitor would know all about it – bound to, isn't he?" added Neil, helping the idea along.

"I suppose there's no harm in that," decided Sir Henry at last, bolstered by the general feeling. "She'd be pleased to know we're looking after her interests."

"Exactly." Neil glanced pointedly at the phone.

"Of course, my dear fellow, I mean, lady," amended Sir Henry in confusion, remembering Sally's revelation about his disguise.

He cleared his throat, switched on his mobile and dialled. "Is that Andrew? Henry hah...Not Henry hah, just Henry – Sir Henry. Oh, I see, you'll put me on to him. Thank you, my dear. Hello? Sorry to trouble you out of hours, my dear fellow. Just want to check on our rental holdings. Yes, the village shop. Can you tell me who owns the leasehold these days? Yes, I'll hold on."

He held his hand over the receiver while he carried on his conversation. "There you are. No messing about. We'll soon get this settled. Hello? That was quick." His voice grew more confident. "Yes, I know I passed some of them over to my dear wife when we got married. You say this wasn't included at the time. Excellent."

He turned triumphantly to the others. "There you are, I told you so." There was a sudden confused babble at the other end. "Yes, still here, what's that you say?" His face turned pale, and he grabbed at the table for support. "It was...what? Added at a later date? Good God! Are you certain? Are you saying that my wife owns the lease on the village shop as well?"

At his words, the smiles of pleasure around him were wiped off instantly, as the significance of his news sank in. William stared dumbly at Neil who turned consolingly to his brother.

"Can this be true?" Albert swallowed, unable to take it in.

"Oh, Pa, what have you done?" Sally clung to William. "Don't you see? Now you've exposed that awful Clive and made her look an idiot, she's getting her own back by helping that wretched Foxey get rid of our village shop!"

"Over my dead body!" thundered Sir Henry. Then as he realised the absurdity of his outburst, he sat back deflated. "What are we going to do?"

After a pause, he turned pathetically to William. "You seem to be an intelligent young man - what would you do?"

"I know it sounds a bit crazy," offered William apologetically, "but there must be some way of diverting her attention onto something else to make her forget all about getting rid of the shop." He turned to the others. "Isn't there anything we can think of that might do the trick?"

They glanced at each other, then hopefully at Neil, as the man with the ideas.

"It's no good looking at me," he confessed. "I don't know what makes her tick. Let's look at this from a different angle like. Tell me, Sir Henry, what would you say her greatest ambition would be in life?"

"Well apart from searching high and low for a suitable young idiot to put money into the estate, I really couldn't say."

There was a concerted groan.

"Of course," he reflected, "she's always been potty about women's lib. Then of course she did cut up when someone else was made President of the local Women's Forum she's got her eye on. I tell you it made our life pretty unbearable at the time."

"That's right." Hettie came to life. "I remember that. They couldn't stand the thought of her bossing them about so they picked on someone she hated the sight of, just for larks. Oh, I'm sorry, Sir Henry – I forgot."

"I see, as bad as that? Well, I can't say I blame them. She's getting quite well known for spreading sweetness and light. In that case," Sir Henry sighed and hoisted himself up, "If there's nothing else I can help you with, I'd better be getting along. Good night to you all."

He took one look at their dejected faces, nodded his head sadly, and took his leave.

"Yes, good night, Sir Henry," replied Albert absently, trying to come to terms with the dreadful news, as his dreams lay shattered around him.

After a while, Sally got up miserably. "I think I'll follow Dad and see if he's all right."

For once, even Neil could think of nothing he could say, and after glancing at Hettie who was trying to console the forlorn figure of Albert, then at William who shook his head in resignation, he decided, "Well, that seems to be that. I vote we wrap it up, and talk it over tomorrow and see if anyone can come up with some fresh ideas."

Chapter Ten
William Has an Idea

"Come on, it can't be as bad as all that," Neil viewed their glum faces, as he tried to raise their spirits next morning.

"Couldn't be worse," retorted Albert despondently. He surveyed the empty street outside and found it difficult to believe that yesterday people were fighting to get in the store. "I don't mind for myself – it's all the other people like Hettie who have supported me – and what's going to happen about young William here?"

"Don't worry about me," offered William, hearing his name mentioned. "I'll find something."

"I'm sure you will," encouraged Hettie brightly. "You can always give me a hand with the pigs."

"That's kind of you," said William hastily, "but I'm sure something will turn up."

Coming to his rescue, Neil reminded Albert, "What about that job with Newman you were talking about the other night. Is he still looking for someone? He might be worth trying."

"You're right – I'll go and see him right away," Albert decided, relieved at something he could do to help him forget his own immediate problems. Fortified by his new mission, he made resolutely for the door.

"Don't trouble on my account," cried William after him, alarmed at what Sally might think, but he was too late.

He needn't have worried. In less than half an hour Albert was back, his face looking like thunder. "D'you know what?" He stood there shaking his head in bemused wonder.

"No, what?" they chorused.

"That idiot Newman wouldn't listen to a thing I said. He actually tried to make out that the wretched fellow wasn't such a bad chap as I made out – 'a square all-rounder' – I believe is the extraordinary phrase he used. Yes, that obnoxious builder he was talking about. I ask you," he repeated seeing the disbelief on their faces, "that awful fellow, what's his name?" His face turned red in an effort to get the words out.

"Fred Foxey," prompted Hettie anxiously, alarmed at his reaction.

"Yes, it turned out, of course, that the real reason behind it all is Foxey has promised a whacking great order for his security alarms, if he goes ahead with some crafty tourist scheme he's planning," he snorted.

"Didn't he seem worried our beautiful high street would be turned into a hideous holiday park – and without his help we're in danger of losing our own village shop?" demanded Hettie fiercely.

"No." Albert hunched his shoulders dejectedly. "He had the nerve to say we mustn't stand in the way of progress."

"Spoken like a true marketing man," commented Neil drily. "It's happening all the time where I come from, and we had a crooked planning officer to contend with – at least you've been spared that. This needs thinking about. We'll have to sit down and find another way to scotch his plans."

"I'm sorry about the shop, Uncle," sympathised William, touched by his plight. "After all the hard work you've put into it and just as it was beginning to pay off, too, with all those orders coming in. It's ironic when you think about it." Then he brightened up. "At least I won't have to be polite to that man-eater, Veronica anymore."

"Oh, don't say that," Hettie argued out of loyalty to Albert. "I'm sure she must be quite a nice girl underneath. She just needs a bit of understanding."

"From a distance," added William with feeling.

"What a shame he's like that," pursued Hettie, letting her imagination run riot. "What a difference he could have made to the village, when it's crying out for funds. Like that poor old village hall of ours, for instance, it'll fall down soon, at the rate it's going, and then where will our Women's Forum be?"

"Really? Is that where they hold their meetings then?" asked Neil, looking suddenly interested.

"Ever since it was built," Hettie thought back, "let me see, some twenty odd years ago. It's time they pulled it down and built a new one, of course – but who's got the money?"

"Wait a minute. If we somehow managed to persuade Newman to contribute, and say it was all Lady C's idea, they might change their opinion of her," argued William, thinking aloud. "That might get her mind off this shop business – she'd be in her element."

"That's right," took up Neil, coming to life. "William, I believe you've got it."

"And how do we do that?" demanded Hettie, bringing them down to earth.

Albert coughed. "Well, it's funny you should say that."

"Yes?" prompted Neil hopefully.

"Well, after all that hogwash about Foxey, he did have the decency to remember about the job I asked him about – for William."

"You spoke, William?" asked Neil courteously, after the spluttering that followed.

"Just something gone down the wrong way. I hope you didn't take him up on it?"

"I didn't need to," Albert beamed.

"Oh, that's good."

"No, he came straight out and said the offer still stands, and you can start by delivering some of those security devices Foxey ordered. And while you're at it, you can sound him out about the village hall. There you are my boy, at least there's something good to come out of the whole miserable business. Otherwise, I'd be feeling personally responsible for ruining your chances just when you need it. It doesn't matter about me, I've just had a lot of fun doing something I've enjoyed doing, eh Het?"

"Oh, Bert you soft old thing, it's what you always wanted."

William looked away uncomfortably as Hettie dabbed at her face and blew her nose.

"Then you'll do it, will you?" asked Albert clearing his throat noisily.

"Oh, all right," William said reluctantly, hoping Sally would never hear about it. "When do I start?"

"Well let's see." Albert glanced up at the clock. "He's expecting a delivery any time now, so you'd better be going."

"Don't forget to have a good look around while you're there," called out Neil after him. "The more we know about that character, the better."

"Why don't you ask the receptionist – she might be able to help you," suggested Albert helpfully.

"And anything else you want to know, if she fancies you," grinned Neil, as the door closed behind him. "Hello, what's that he said?"

Hettie was puzzled. "Sounded like, 'poles apart'. I wonder what he meant?"

Luckily, he didn't have to put it to the test as it appeared the dreaded Veronica was away looking up an old female chum she knew back in high school. But having survived that particular hurdle, he was about to confront an even bigger one as far as Sally was concerned.

Arriving later to find out the latest news on her way to one of her lessons, Sally was just in time to see William cross the road carrying a box and knock on the door of the house opposite. A few minutes later the door opened, and a young girl eyed William up and down before ushering him in with an extra special welcoming smile. Coming as it did on top of his previous encounters with the fair sex, it acted on Sally like an open knife wound.

"Who shall I say called?" The young girl simpered at the sight of him.

William kept his eyes fixed studiously over her head. "I've just come to deliver some security items for a Mr Foxey – he is expecting them, I understand."

"Oh yes, he's busy right now. Would you like to wait?"

"If I may." Inside, William cast a quick look around the hallway. Behind a closed door on the left he could hear a muffled drone of voices. As he spoke, he pretended to drop his handkerchief, and scooping to pick it up he tried to pick up the thread of the conversation inside.

"There's a waiting room just in here, if you like," the receptionist invited, brushing past him as she led the way. William coughed and followed her into a dingy waiting room, sitting down hurriedly to forestall any further overtures on her part.

"Just as you like," she pouted. "There's a newspaper and magazines - unless there's anything else you want?" Piqued at his lack of lack of interest, she murmured coyly, "Call me if you want, my name's Sybil."

"Er, no, that will be fine, thank you," said William hastily.

"Suit yourself. I'll tell him as soon as he's free."

After the door closed behind her he waited a few minutes until her footsteps died away, then opened his briefcase and fetched out a curious looking stethoscope which he pressed against the particle board wall, and listened intently through a pair of miniature headphones.

He was just able to make out a couple of disjointed phrases including the question, "What time?" and "Everyone here on Thursday 2.30 sharp", then the scrape of chairs and a voice saying, "What does he want?" At the sound of returning footsteps William just had time to stuff the equipment away before the girl returned.

"He'll see you now," she sniffed, put out by his lack of interest. "This way."

As he followed her in a short scruffy looking man with beady eyes got up and eyed him up and down suspiciously, before waving him to a seat. "Hang about, you're new, aren't you?"

Trying not to notice the squinting eyes, and anxious not to arouse too many questions, William did his best to appear casual. "Just helping out. I understand you asked these to be delivered right away, Mr Foxey? I hope they're what you wanted."

Fred Foxey gave the boxes a curt glance and dropped them on the table, apparently satisfied. "Yes, they'll do." He inspected William more closely. "Here, your face looks familiar – where have I seen you before – are you one of Newman's lot?"

"That's right, I've only started recently." William let his face relax. "Is there anything else we can help you with, while I'm here?"

"What's your name?" asked Foxey, still suspicious.

Deciding it was best to keep to the truth where possible, William told him.

"William Bridge? I know you – doesn't your uncle run the village store? What's the game then, why are you working for the Yank next door?"

"Money, that's what," said William quickly, adopting a discontented expression. "Don't get enough of it, do I? Mean old so- and- so," he added, hoping to sound convincing. "Besides, the old place is on the rocks, innit?"

An evil smirk appeared on the other's face. "Is that so? Want to earn some more, eh?"

Feigning indifference, William allowed a grudging note to creep into his voice. "Could be – what's in it for me?"

A calculated look of satisfaction appeared briefly on the other's face. "Stick around, and keep your ears close to the ground. I might make it worth it, depending on what I find out across the road. Get me?"

"Right." William nodded in understanding. "No skin off my nose."

"Right then." Foxey stood up, indicating the conversation was at an end. "Goodbye young man, I hope to hear more from you."

"Oh, you will," William promised him. "You certainly will, Mr Foxey. Thanks, I'll see my own way out."

"Well, how did you get on, son?" asked Ed Newman eagerly as he reported back. "He's one of my best customers, you know." His voice took on a fresh note of appeal. "Is he likely to want anything more? We could do with some more or- ders right now – you limeys need wakening up, I can see that."

William appeared diffident. "Not at the mo- ment, I'm afraid, but he seemed quite interested."

"Good, good."

"I know our methods may sometimes seem rather different to you over here," began William cautiously, wondering how he might lead up to it, "but have you tried setting up any kind of local exhibition centre to show off some of your security systems? It wouldn't need a massive staff to look after it, you know."

Newman chewed over the suggestion, then shook his head regretfully. "I sure would love to, but think of the cost of the building and everything – I've got to justify anything like that to the Board you know. Can't be done on the back of a dollar."

"It needn't be all that expensive," said William persuasively. "There are one or two places I could think of you could hire that wouldn't involve any building work, they just need to be brought up to scratch - like a village hall, for instance. Why we've even got one just down the road – you wouldn't even have to rent it outright, you could share it with all kinds of local organisations."

"Is that so?" mused Newman, his eyes lighting up at the prospect. "Gee, that sounds great. How do I go about it?"

Trying not to sound too enthusiastic, William shrugged. "I could take you down and introduce you myself, if you like. I know the Vicar and all the people who run it - everyone knows everyone in a small village like this."

"You do? Why, what are we waiting for? Let's do it. Tell me, Willie, you don't mind me calling you that? No? Good. What kind of outfits use the village hall these days?"

"Let me see. There's a dancing class, gymnastics, bridge sessions, you name it - and regular events like the Women's Forum…" He broke off in simulated surprise, "But of course, I believe your friend, Lady Courtney, is a member of that. It's very popular, I understand."

"What, my old friend, Margery? I didn't know that."

William leaned closer, as is if imparting some confidential news. "As a matter of fact, we're hoping to get her elected as our new President. The present one is stepping down – let's see, I think they're holding a meeting this week."

"That's great. Wait till I see her."

"Of course," William lowered his voice. "There's always quite a bit of competition for the position – it's considered quite an honour, you know."

"Is that so? Is there any way I can help my old friend?"

William hesitated, as if considering the idea for the first time. "Well, since you're an old friend and willing to help and all that, there is one way I can think of, but I don't know if I should mention it."

"Well, shoot, Willie, shoot," insisted Newman, warming to the possibility.

William took a deep breath. "It would mean an awful lot to the members if someone smartened the place up a bit. And even better, if they let it be known they are willing to become a sponsor - as an old friend of the family, if you know what I mean. It would boost her chances no end."

"Why, I'd be only too glad to, for my old friend Margery. Consider it done, Willie, and thank you for telling me. How do we go about it?"

Thinking it over, William slapped his forehead. "Of course, why didn't I think of that before. Why don't we get you to come and give a talk to the meeting as a guest speaker, and make an announcement about becoming a sponsor at the same time?"

"Gee, yes, but what do I talk about? I'm not much of an expert on what women like to hear."

William seemed surprised at the question. "Why, on security in the home, of course, what else? It gives you a chance to spread the word about your company, and get yourself talked about into the bargain."

Ed Newman slapped him on the back. "Gee, that's pure genius. Let me know when you need me there. I can see we'll have to make you a Vice-President before long."

"Oh, I wouldn't say that, Mr Newman," said William modestly. "Only too pleased to help an old friend of the family."

"Say, leave out the Mr Newman stuff – call me Edward."

"Glad to, Mr Newman, I mean, Edward," said William hastily.

"Forget the Edward bit," enthused his genial host, escorting him to the front door. "Call me 'Ed', Willie boy, now you're becoming one of us."

Chapter Eleven
Thrashing It Out

Feeling optimistic at the way the way things were going, William called into the shop to make his report. About to push open the door he was startled when a hand emerged and yanked him in, after the owner of said hand took a cautionary glance up and down the high street.

"Quick, inside, before that blasted Cuthbert comes back." Reassured the coast was clear, Neil relaxed his grip and mopped his face. "He's been dogging my heels all morning. I can't move without him chasing me. Now, what's the latest?"

William filled him in, and Neil quickly grasped the significance of his visit. "Why, that's great!"

By now, attracted by his enthusiasm, Albert and Hettie hurried over and had the story repeated, with Sally following up reluctantly behind.

"You realise what this means," Neil told the others. "Now William here has got the lowdown on their plans at last, we have a chance to out-smart them."

"How do we do that?" asked Albert eagerly.

"Why, now we know the layout of the place, all we've got to do is to get inside again when they're not looking and find out what they're up to."

"How on earth d'you think you're going to do that?" asked William, thanking his lucky stars his part was now over, and he was well out of it.

Neil turned to him in surprise and rubbed his shoulder affectionately. "Why, you don't need to fool me, my boy. I knew you couldn't wait to get back inside - I didn't want to spoil your fun."

"Me?" William was appalled. "You don't seriously expect me to try and get into that place again, after all that?"

"Won't that be dangerous?" Hettie wanted to know. "We don't want any harm to come to the boy." Sally was equally opposed to the idea, much to William's relief.

For a moment, Neil seemed surprised at their reaction. "How else are we going to do it? William is the obvious choice. He knows the layout of the place, and they're used to the sight of him – so what's the objection?"

"And how d'you think they're going to let me in, when they're all set to hold their meeting in private?" demanded William triumphantly.

For a moment, Neil was stumped. "There must be some way of getting in that house without being noticed," he mused.

"No doubt he can get that receptionist to help – I notice they were getting very pally together," broke in Sally frostily.

"I didn't have anything to do with her," protested William heatedly. "You've got it all wrong."

But Sally had heard enough. "You go in there, and I'll never speak to you again," she burst out, and with a sob she rushed out of the shop.

After an awkward pause, Neil put an arm around William. "Don't worry, leave her to cool down, she'll come round. Now listen William, we're relying on you. Unless we find out what their game is your Uncle Albert here will have to sell up, you do realise that. You've simply got to get back in there. Now," he fished out the stethoscope from William's pocket and threw it away.

"This is no use to us any more – what we need is proof. We need some means of recording their conversation so we can nail them, or at the very least find out what they're up to." He paced up and down. "Now we know we're on the right track - we've got to organise something going on at the same time to lull their suspicions, so they'll feel we're not interested in what they're doing. But what?" He wheeled round hopefully. "Got any ideas?"

With a groan, William wrestled with the thought of Sally's ultimatum while he did his best to sort his ideas out.

"I suppose Ed Newman might have something we could use," he said trying to concentrate, in an effort to ease his aching heart, "but that's not the problem. What are we going to organise to distract them, and how do we get in there?"

Neil snapped his fingers. "Why, you told us yourself – we get this Women's Forum, or whatever you call them, to hold their meeting the same afternoon and elect Lady C as President, that should take their minds off it all – and of course, this Mavis Poxey of yours is bound to go along as a member to keep an eye on things for them, which would be one less of the gang to worry about."

"Foxey," corrected Hettie automatically.

Albert shuddered at the mention of her name, but found himself caught up in the excitement of the drama unfolding. "Go on, then what?"

"And how do we smuggle ourselves in again without them knowing?" demanded William heatedly. "Wave a magic wand or something? He's not called Foxy for nothing."

"Wait a minute." Hettie called the meeting to order. "What time did you say the meeting was going to start?"

"2:30 sharp," answered William promptly, casting his mind back.

"And what day, did you say?" chimed in Albert.

"Thursday."

They looked at each other, struck by the same thought.

"Are we talking about the day after tomorrow?" Albert voiced their anxiety.

William nodded, brightening at the thought it meant they couldn't manage to work out a plan in that short time, which left him off the hook.

"The day after tomorrow?" Neil questioned thoughtfully. "We'd better put our skates on then. Come on, think. How are we going to get young William in, without anyone noticing?"

"Why me?" William asked passionately. "Why does it always have to be me?"

Neil gave a short, amused laugh. "Why, you don't seriously expect any of us to manage it, do you, when I've got Constable Cuthbert breathing down my neck every time I stick my head out of the door?"

"I've just remembered something," Hettie spoke excitedly. "That receptionist goes to lunch at midday."

"What do you expect me to do about it – kidnap her? That's the first thing they'll notice when the others arrive for the meeting," scoffed William sarcastically, doing his best to kill the idea stone dead.

"No, but if we could engage her attention for a short while just as she comes out, while some-one slips in behind her back..." Hettie continued stubbornly, looking meaningly at William.

"Of course," interrupted Neil, taken with the notion. "Let me see, she's young and would fall for anything free. I know, why don't you ask her to take part in a survey, Hettie, when she comes out, and offer her a new brand of make-up for taking part? Hey, how about that?"

"And how do I get out again?" William wanted to know, looking reproachfully at Hettie.

Neil brushed that aside as unimportant. "Don't worry about that. I'll slip out of the Women's Forum meeting before it finishes and wait until the meeting breaks up, and get you out somehow. The most important thing is to find out what they're up to – are we agreed?"

The others nodded and avoided looking at William.

"I think there is one thing you've all forgotten," he reminded them with rising hope.

"What's that?" Neil sounded unconcerned.

"Where do I hide once I get in there, so I can hear what's going on?"

"Ah," Neil was saved from answering by the ringing of the shop bell, and Sir Henry stuck his head in.

"I say, am I interrupting anything? Just thought I'd pop in and see how everything is, don't you know."

Appealing for support, William played his trump card. "Fine, except they're trying to get me to hide in Foxey's cottage across the road while he's having a meeting so's I can hear everything that's going on, that's all."

"Oh, you mean that dealer chap." Sir Henry frowned in an effort to concentrate. "D'you know, something occurred to me just then when you said that, I wonder what it was?" Suddenly a light of unaccustomed intelligence shone on the noble baronet's countenance. "I know, it's something about the history of that place. Now, what the deuce was it?"

"Don't tell me, let me guess - it was a gambling den in Henry V111's time," offered Hettie brightly.

"It was probably burnt down in the Great Fire," countered William darkly.

"No, but it was about that time," mused Sir Henry. "It was something to do with smuggling, I seem to remember."

"What, silks and finery and that sort of thing?" hazarded Albert.

"No, it was a tavern," corrected William automatically, a vague memory surfacing of a conversation he'd had with Malcolm about the history of the village, realising too late he'd said too much.

"By George, I believe you're right, well done." Sir Henry coughed apologetically, remembering in time he'd come to question William's recent behaviour towards his daughter. "Which reminds me, I've got a bone to pick with you, my boy. What have you done to upset my Sal?"

"She seems to think I'm stuck on that wretched receptionist across the road – just because I delivered some security stuff for Ed Newman. It's not true, but she won't believe me. And now they want me to go into that house again when she's there – what am I supposed to do?" he appealed miserably.

Sir Henry looked across to the others, and they nodded energetically.

"He can't possibly duck out at this stage." Neil was quite definite. "We're relying on William to pull it off. The whole operation depends on him – otherwise we're sunk. You tell him, Sir Henry. He'll listen to you. Surely Sally must understand that?"

"Listen to an old man, my boy." Sir Henry placed an arm around William's shoulders. "There comes a time in everyone's life when we have to face up to unpleasant decisions and make the right choice. Heaven knows, I've had to do it myself enough times – and a right pig's ear I've made of it on occasions. Hrm, that's by the by. But this time, we both know they're right, don't we? It all depends on you, my boy. Look, I tell you what, you do your best to pull it off, and I'll have another word with Sally and try and make her understand – how about that?"

"Will you?" William raised his head hopefully.

"Of course."

In the pause that followed, Albert surfaced out of his usual mental fog, still grappling with the thought about the history of the cottage. "I'm sorry," he questioned, slightly confused. "I'm sure the fact it was a tavern must be of some vital importance. But how does that help us?"

"Don't you see?" appealed Sir Henry. He noted their lack of response with some surprise, and began to enlighten them. "In the old days, they established some sort of smuggling run, don't you know, to avoid the customs."

"You'll be telling us next that they built a secret passage up to the inn, to smuggle the contraband in," scoffed William distractedly.

Sir Henry looked impressed. "How did you know that? My word, you're quick off the mark, my boy."

"He is that," agreed Neil excitedly. "Now, what we need to know now, Sir Henry, is where it comes out. Dammit, that might be the answer to all our problems!"

"Good gracious, I wish I knew," admitted Sir Henry candidly. "Why, I could make a fortune out of it, conducting guide tours around the place, couldn't I?" He laughed, then seeing that his information had fallen flat, he edged out through the door, deciding he'd postpone his chat with William until later. "Well, I'm glad I was able to help you. Cheerio."

Neil tried one last shot. "There's no way of getting into it from the cottage, I suppose?"

"Sorry, my boy, afraid I've no idea." Then he poked his head in again. "Though I did hear someone mention once there's a secret hiding place behind a bookcase somewhere."

"What?" William sat up with a jerk.

"You spoke?" enquired Neil courteously.

"No," mumbled William.

"I fancy that remark of Sir Henry's struck a chord, did it not?"

Deciding to come clean, William admitted reluctantly, "I believe there was a bookcase in his office when I was there."

"Where, no doubt, the celebrated meeting is due to take place?"

"Oh, all right," groaned William in torment. "I'll do it."

"Good man, I knew we could rely on you. Now that we've got that settled," Neil went on briskly, "all we need to do now is to get Lady C elected in time for the next meeting of the Women's Forum, and make sure Ed is free to give his talk. By the way, do we know when that is? Hettie, you're a member, aren't you?"

"Usually it's on a Saturday when they can be sure everyone is likely to be available, but I suppose if it's an emergency, we could bring it forward."

"And who's the best person to talk to about it?"

"Well, there is your aunt, William dear," offered Hettie hesitantly. "After all, she practically runs the place back stage. Do you think she would be persuaded to help?"

For the first time, a smile flitted across William's face. "She would if we tell her Ed Newman has agreed to help pay towards the cost of repairs to the village hall in return for using it as an exhibition centre."

"Do you think that's likely," said Neil doubtfully. "It means spending a lot of bucks."

"He's already agreed to do it," confirmed William absently, wondering if Sir Henry would be able to put in a good word with Sally as he had promised.

Neil slapped his forehead in admiration. "William, you're a marvel. What are we waiting for – let's go and ask her."

However, Aunt Ethel was not amused when she answered the door to their insistent ringing.

"What do you want?" she answered, somewhat flustered, annoyed at being caught in the middle of her housework in her overalls. "Can't a body be left to do her work properly without all this racketing?" Then catching sight of William,

"Oh, it's you – finished early, have we? Some sort of half day, is it?"

"Nothing like that, Aunt," said William quickly. "We've come to ask a favour. Can we come in?"

She gave a quick up and down look at Neil, dwelling suspiciously on his attire. "I suppose so," she said grudgingly. "You'd better go in the front room while I get tidied up."

When she heard what they had to say, she looked them up and down sternly. "Are you expecting me to condone your antics in some kind of bribery, is that it?"

"Well, I wouldn't put it like that exactly," said Albert anxiously.

"It means you get the hall repaired for next to nothing," William put it bluntly.

"Why didn't you say so in the first place, you great noonie!" snapped Aunt Ethel. "I'd put her Ladyship up for Prime Minister for less than that."

"Then you'll do it?" beamed Neil enthusiastically. "I could kiss you for that!"

"You'll do no such thing," bridled Aunt Ethel, stepping back and eyeing him suspiciously. "You keep your distance."

"But how can you persuade the others to vote for her Ladyship, Ethel?" quavered Albert nervously.

"I'll see to that, never you mind," she promised. "Now away with you while I finish my housework, the lot of you." As she shooed them out, she gave her broom a vigorous shake, leaving them in no doubt that the business of appointing the next President was as good as settled.

Chapter Twelve
Ed's Arsenal

Neil wasted no time the next morning to start the ball rolling. He charged into the shop, nearly tripping over his dress, and found William still recovering from the shock of seeing Sally's uncompromising message left on his mobile, making him depressed and uncertain, wondering if her father had had a chance to talk to her.

After shaking him to get his attention Neil weighed in breezily, "Wake up, William, old lad. It's time for action. We've got to nip in next door and sock it to Newman about the chat he's going to give. There's nothing like a spot of good news to start the day off, eh?"

William sat up hopefully at his words, feeling as if he'd survived ten rounds in the ring and the seconds were giving him a life-saving respite. "So you're coming as well, are you? I thought you were keeping well out of it."

A pained expression crossed Neil's face. "Cor blimey, talk sense. Someone's got to stay here and organise things, it stands to reason. Why, you've got the easy bit, chatting up Ed and the gorgeous Veronica, what more do you want?"

"Oh no, don't say she's back?" William looked anxious. "That's all I need. I thought she was away visiting someone."

"Well, you'll soon find out, won't you, now's your chance. Off you go, and give your Ed my regards."

As he pushed William out the door, he suddenly caught sight of a figure crossing the road, and drew back electrified.

"Oh, my Gawd, did you see who that was – it's him!"

Following the pointed finger, William was puzzled. "You mean that man who's just gone into Foxey's place? Who's he? Do you know him?"

"Know him?" Neil sounded shell shocked. "He's the flaming swine who set me up in the first place! If it wasn't for him, I wouldn't be dressed up as a perishing pantomime queen hiding from the rossers, would I?"

"But what did he do?" William for once forgot his own problems in the face of this unexpected mystery.

"He sold our market pitch down the river to the local builder, didn't he?"

"But how did he do that?" William said, trying to grope his way through his uncle's cockney slang.

Neil explained patiently. "I'm telling you. One of the local villains up our way who describes himself loosely as a builder – not what I'd call him - slipped him a bung to get planning permission, so's he could build all over our market square that's been there for bleeding hundreds of years, that's all." He fumed. "And if I know Bernie – he's doing it all over again on your own doorstep."

"But couldn't you have stopped him?"

Neil laughed bitterly. "No, because when we tried, that so-and-so Bernie had me up for assault, and got me tagged an' all."

"But he couldn't do that without some sort of evidence."

"Well, I must admit I did paste him one when he called me a liar – what else could I do?" asked Neil reasonably.

"Quite," said William hastily.

"Mind you, it took half a dozen of the rossers to get me in the van," his uncle added proudly. "Anyway, that's neither here nor there. If we want to put a stop to their crafty tricks, we'd better not hang about – you get cracking and do your stuff. I shouldn't bother trying to tell Ed what we know about that lot though – from what you told me, he'll never believe you."

"Right," said William thoughtfully. "I'll see what I can do."

Adjusting himself to the new situation, he went over in his mind all they had discussed on his previous visit as he made his way to Newman's cottage.

As the door opened he saw to his relief that it was Newman himself who answered the door.

"Hi! Come in, Willie, and spill the beans. What's new?"

Despite the beaming welcome, William looking around cautiously as he stepped inside, half expecting to be pounced on.

"Veronica not back yet?" he asked nervously, getting ready to retreat before the usual ear-splitting howl signalled her presence.

Ed Newman gazed at him in sympathy. "Gee, I'm sorry, I know how it is with you young love birds – can't wait to get together again, eh? No, I'm expecting her any moment.

I thought that was her when you came - guess she must have got held up somewhere. Tell you what though, I've just got a new bottle of bour-bon in that might help to pass the time away. What d'you say, Willie?"

Not wishing to offend, William agreed politely, casting a quick glance at his watch, wondering how soon they could get down to business. He needn't have bothered for Ed beat him to it by coming right out about it, without beating about the bush.

"Have you fixed it with my old friend, Margery?" he asked eagerly, as he splashed out a generous measure, and handed it over.

"No, but I'm told it's all been arranged," said William truthfully, remembering the determined expression on his Aunt Ethel's face.

"Hey, that's great! When do we start?"

"Well, we're hoping to arrange it for Thursday afternoon," began William, taken aback at the other's eager reaction. "I'm sorry, it's rather short notice - I hope I'm not rushing you."

"Rushing me?" gurgled Ed Newman, thumping his chest apologetically. "And there was I, all set to work my socks off to get the show on the road. I thought you were going to say at least next month or so – that's amazing." He chuckled. "That'll teach that young Vee to believe her old dad. I won't tell you what she said about you being slow to get started." He broke off hastily, "Say, let me freshen up that glass."

William tried to cover up his glass, too late. "That's fine. Er, d'you think that'll give you time to think up what to say at the meeting?"

Ed Newman patted his shoulder. "Hey, you can stop worrying about that. Say, I've got my writers back home working on it right now – don't give it another thought."

"Right, that's fine, fine." He got to his feet a trifle unsteadily, hanging onto his chair as the accumulated effects of his host's drinks caught up with him.

He gazed owlishly at the other, as the room began to swing around him, and for a moment he tried to remember why he was there. "I know." He held up his hand, struck by a sudden thought. "You could take along one or two of your gadgets to give them some idea of the kind of security systems you have."

"That's a great idea, Willie. Say, while you're here, why don't I show you some of them?"

William looked surprised and pleased, as if the thought had never occurred to him. "I'd like that very much – are you sure I'm not taking up your time?"

But Newman was already leading the way, explaining over his shoulder as they went. "No sirree, it'll give me great pleasure to show off my toys. Besides," he chuckled, amused by a sudden thought, "Vee would never forgive me if I let you go before she got back – I'd never hear the last of it."

William winced at the thought, and hurried on behind. As they emerged at the back of the cottage he glanced around, puzzled. All he could remember from his previous visit was a tiny little ramshackle shed at the bottom of garden - hardly a fitting place to show off anything.

Seeing his bewilderment, Ed Newman dug him in the ribs. "That fooled you, didn't it? Follow me, I've got this snug little hidy hole down the garden."

As they rounded a spreading holly bush, William blinked at the sight before them. In place of the well remembered shack was a compact brick built office, ringed by a reinforced fence and a forbidding cluster of security cameras. A powerful beam sprang into life with a blaze of light as they approached.

"How about that – neat eh?" crowed Ed, fishing out a bunch of keys.

"It certainly is," agreed William faintly.

"Take an army and a Sherman tank to get through this little lot," nodded his host, well satisfied. "This way, mind the barbed wire." He proceeded to unlock first an outer barrier, then a heavily metal plated entrance door that looked more like an opening into a bank's vault.

Locking the door behind them, Ed Newman flung out a hand, "Welcome to the snug – what d'you think of that?"

"It's amazing," said William, shaking his head in an effort to concentrate, as he took it all in. "But you haven't been here all that long – how did you manage to get this built in such a short time?"

"Just good old U.S know-how," offered Ed modestly. "What d'you think of that little lot?" He gestured to rows and rows of weird looking devices spread around the room, stacked up in piles, and filling up all the available space on the shelves.

"Great." William took a closer look, not quite sure what he should say next. "Er, can you explain what they are for?"

"Why sure." Ed Newman gestured at the array of small objects dotted around. "These little gizmos are bugs, the sort you fix on phones and things to tap in on conversations – industrial espionage they call it. The larger beasts are for listening in from a way off – we've got 'em all, you name it, buddy boy."

Pulling himself together, William checked the time, anxious not to hang about with Veronica in the offing. "I'm sure they'll be thrilled with any of this – has anyone else seen it?"

"No, sir, this is top secret stuff - we don't show this to any old Tom, Dick or Harry, as you would say over here." Ed was quite definite, and reflected, "only to our more important customers, of course – like my old friend, Fred Foxey, who's one of my big customers."

At the mention of his name, William jumped and nervously dropped an odd shaped fountain pen he'd picked up by mistake. "I say, I'm sorry, someone must have left this behind."

"No worries, son," beamed Ed, putting his arm around William's shoulders. "That's what you're meant to think. See here," he picked it up proudly, "this little marvel is the prize of my collection. You'd think, looking at it for the first time, it's just an ordinary bog standard fountain pen, wouldn't you?"

William nodded politely, not wanting to spoil his enthusiasm.

"Well, you couldn't be more wrong. See here, this little beauty only has to be pointed at someone, and it will not only record every whisper of their conversation, but this tiny lens at the end will film everything they do, as well. Good, eh? I thought that would grab you."

William eyed the object wistfully. He was dying to slip it in his pocket, but was caught in a quandary. After hearing his enemy, Foxy Fred, was Ed's favourite customer, he knew he had an uphill battle on his hands trying to explain why he wanted it.

Newman would never believe Foxey was up to anything fishy. He groaned inwardly in frustration. His course of action was already decided however by a faint helloo from the direction of the cottage.

"Why, that must be Vee," cried Ed Newman joyfully. He put the pen back on the stand, killing off William's hopes of getting his hands on it. "Enough of this. I guess you can't wait to see her again, eh?" He nudged his young friend gleefully.

"No," accepted William hollowly. He tried to hide his disappointment and pulled himself together. "Well, thanks for the drinks, sir, I mean, Ed." He looked at his watch hurriedly. "Gosh, I've just remembered an urgent appointment..."

"Gee, that reminds me, talking about drinks," Ed grabbed his arm. "I don't suppose you can cast your mind back to that break-in you had?"

"Break-in?" queried William feverishly. "Can't say I do, now if you'll excuse me…"

"Gee, I certainly do," went on his host, still clutching his sleeve, preventing him from leaving. "I woke up in that pig sty with a hangover you could shake a stick at, and blundered into the shop just as you had that shake down, remember?"

"Did you? I mean I really must go now."

"How I got into that state I can't remember," confessed Ed, disregarding his attempts. "All I do recall is getting hold of a honey of a drink. I seem to remember your Aunt Isobel called it 'Ferdie's medicine'. Jeepers, I'd do anything to get my hands on that beautiful stuff – I'd die for it."

"You would?" said William thickly, trying to concentrate, as he searched his befuddled memory for the elusive reason why they were keeping it a secret.

"You name it," promised Ed simply.

"Well, er," began William, warming to the thought, "I believe I did hear somewhere that you could get it at a vet's."

Ed Newman drew back incredulously. "What's that you say - at a dawg's clinic? Are you serious?"

"Yes," said William solemnly. "It's a well kept secret. Now, about that promise, do you think I could borrow one of your gadgets for a day or two, just on loan, as it were."

"A dawg clinic?" repeated Ed wonderingly. "Jeepers, what sort of an outfit is that?"

"Just someone Hettie knows," pleaded William, looking over his shoulder nervously.

"But, how does he operate? Has he got a still on the side or something? Say what's his name, where can I find him – is he on the run from the cops?"

"No, it's all perfectly respectable – have a word with Hettie, she'll tell you."

"She will? Why that's great, I'll just do that. Willie, you're a swell guy, I'll tell the world. Now, about that gadget," he beamed, "what d'you want? Couple of bugs or earpieces? Help yourself, we've got them all."

"Er, say a few bugs, and could you make it that jolly little pen device as well?"

"Hrm, well as it's you, okay, but you will watch over it, Willie, that's worth a small fortune to me. Here you are."

William took the pen with trembling hands and placed it reverently in his pocket. "I don't know how to thank you, Ed."

"Think nothing of it – you will take care of it, though."

"Don't worry, I will," said William gratefully, casting another uneasy glance up the garden.

"So all I do is ask Hettie, eh?" breathed Ed reverently. "I think I'll do just that."

"Good, good. Only," William hesitated, "you must remember to call it 'Ferdie's' medicine, when you ask her."

"I get it," winked Ed. "Top secret is it? Don't worry, my lips are sealed. You know what? You've just given me the key to a beautiful dream – 'Ferdie's' medicine," he licked his lips in anticipation, "here I come."

"Talking about keys," William reminded him absently, "don't you think we'd better lock up. We don't want anyone breaking in, do we?"

Ed Newman looked at him pityingly. "You don't think I had this specially built so's anything like that could happen? I got all my money locked up in that little old safe over there. Why this is more foolproof than Fort Knox! I defy anyone to bust this open."

"What happens if you happen to get locked in accidentally?" asked William out of polite interest, as they turned to go out.

"Why, that's no problem – you just turn the handle and open it from the inside – that's no problem. But just you try to get in – that's a different ball game all together. See here?" he pointed at a button on the floor just inside the door. "This is my secret weapon – it's a beaut little burglar alarm. I set it every evening, just as I leave. Wanna hear it?"

Before William could say anything, Newman trod on it before closing the door, then tried rattling the handle.

Immediately the peace was shattered by an ear splitting howl of a savage dog that sounded so realistic William jumped into the air, and nearly climbed on the roof in effort to escape.

"Good, eh?" shouted Ed above the din.

As the terrifying roars died away there was an answering yahoo from the cottage, and they saw the distant figure of Veronica waving at them in recognition before hurrying towards them.

Just then there was a bleep from Ed's mobile, and he fished it out and listened, waving William on as he did so. "You go back, Willie. I know you can't wait to see her. Tell Vee I won't be long."

William smiled weakly and sidled round the holly bush until he was out of sight, then he broke into a clumsy sprint to the fence. Before he could manage to clamber over, a couple of slim arms wound themselves around his waist, and the determined honeyed tones of Veronica cooed in his ear.

"Hi! Lover boy, where have you been? I've been thinking of you all day, and here you are dished up on a plate."

Fighting his way out of her clutches, William panted, "Sorry Vee, must dash. I've got a terribly important appointment, and I'm late. Let me go, please!"

"Not before I've said hello properly, lover boy." And before he could free himself, she smothered his face with kisses. "That's for starters – jeepers, you've been drinking with Pa again," she reeled

backed, loosening her hold. "Wait, I haven't finished yet!"

But William had. With a final wrench, he
sprang clear and hoofed it for the safety of
the shop, not stopping for breath until he had
slammed the door behind him and clung to the
counter, panting, his head in his hands. After a
few gasping snorts, he mopped his face and out
of the corner of his eyes he saw a pair of shoes
tapping ominously on the floor in front of him.

Lifting his head, he was confronted by a new
version of Sally, who regarded him with frosty
eyes and set lips.

"Sally!" he smiled fatuously. "Is it really you,
darling? You don't know how much I've missed
you."

"So I see!" she blazed. "It may interest you to
know that my father has been pleading with me
all morning to forgive your outrageous philan-
dering, and after giving you the benefit of the
doubt, I come here and find you at it again, covered with lipstick, and," she bent forward and
sniffed, "and you've been drinking. How could
you!"

"But darling," pleaded William desperately, "I can explain…"

"This is the last straw." She bit her lips. "I never want to see you again. Goodbye."

With a whirl of fury, she stormed out and the door slammed behind her, shattering a pane of glass.

Chapter Thirteen
Sneaking In

Thursday morning started off with two unlucky omens. First, Neil was phoned by a distraught Hettie who told him his dress had been sent off to the laundry by mistake, and she was frantically searching for a replacement. And if that was not enough, it was discovered at the last minute there had been a double booking at the village hall, just as the members of the Women's Forum were waking up to the unwelcome news that their monthly meeting was going to be held that very afternoon, instead of the traditional Saturday opening they had come to expect - which in itself should have been a sign everything was not going to turn out as well as everyone had expected.

Unfortunately, nobody told the new booking clerk who had already given in to a frantic plea from a desperate secretary at the local agricultural show to allow them to use the car park as an overspill on the same afternoon. Consequently, as some of the lady volunteers turned up a trifle flustered, ready to start setting out chairs and opening up the kitchen in preparation for their afternoon meeting, they were faced with the problem of ejecting a medley of farm animals which had wandered into the hall by mistake. By the time they managed to clear up the mess left behind and opened all the windows, they were beginning to have grave doubts as to whether they would have it ready in time for the opening - when they would be faced with the onerous task of electing a new and unpopular president, as well as coping with the demands of a special guest speaker, who ironically would be telling them how to protect their property against intruders.

All this was being relayed to Neil as he stood shivering in his underwear, partly hidden behind the counter at the back of the shop, as he endeavoured to supervise the day's events - breaking off now and then to call up Hettie to enquire somewhat peevishly about the whereabouts of his replacement dress.

He was still in a state of semi-undress when the tinkle of the shop bell caused him to dive for cover, in case it was Cuthbert the bobby tracking him down.

Luckily, it turned out to be William who had been unsuccessfully trying to make sense out of the fountain pen recorder Ed Newman had spoken of in such lyrical terms. After twisting the cap in every conceivable position to try to make it work he had given it up as a bad job, and faced with the perilous dangers of running into Veronica again to get it explained by Ed - the very thought of which brought him out in a cold sweat - he decided to consult Neil as to what he should do about it.

But Neil was in no mood to be bothered with such trivialities in the drama of unfolding events. "Stop waving that thing at me," he cried peevishly. "What I want to know is, where's my dress? Hasn't Hettie found anything I can wear yet? Do you realise what the time is? That meeting across the road is due to start in under an hour, and you're not even ready yet. Where is everyone?"

William decided he'd had enough. After going to all the trouble of getting hold of a recording pen that didn't work, and facing up to a bleak future without Sally, he was in no mood to be told what to do any longer. "It's no good going on to me about it, Neil," he burst out, stung beyond endurance. "I've just about had it up to my neck. As far as I'm concerned, that's it - you can find someone else to do it."

Neil stared at him aghast, all thoughts of his dress forgotten. "Do you know what you're saying? Why the whole success of the scheme depends on you!"

"Why don't you do it then?" demanded William hotly. "You're so full of ideas. If you can disguise yourself as a woman, you can pass yourself off as anything."

"But…but everyone knows me as Aunt Isobel, and your aunt can't go anywhere without a dress, surely you realise that!" Neil pleaded, desperately waving away Hettie who had just appeared in the background, triumphantly holding up a dress.

"You can't back out now, Willie. Why, you're the only one who's been in Foxey's office and knows where everything is, and where to hide. Don't you understand? I've got to stay here and organise everything, otherwise it will all be ruined. If I go anywhere near that place, and that swine Bernie catches sight of me and reports me to the rossers, I'll be back in the nick double quick, and then where will you be?"

Seeing his nephew remained unconvinced, Neil had a sudden inspiration. "Listen, don't you realise? Once we can prove he's up to no good Foxey would never dare go ahead with that development scheme of his, and without those juicy orders coming in, our friend Ed would have to give up his plans and go back to the States taking Veronica with him – now is it a go, or is it a go?"

As the thought sank home, William's eyes lit up, and he clutched Neil's arm feverishly. "I'll do it! I'll do it - when do we start?"

Neil heaved a sigh of relief. "Good man, I knew you would see sense."

"Wait a minute," William remembered, fishing out the fountain pen in a sudden panic, "how the heck do I make this gizmo work to get the proof we need?"

"Is that all you're worrying about. Here," Neil delved into a drawer, and brandished a miniature tape recorder. "While you were gallivanting next door yesterday, I had this sent down from London, in case you didn't manage to come up with anything."

Words almost failed William. "D'you mean to say you made me go through all that palaver, and then get slated by Sally into the bargain, all for nothing?"

"Yes, well, you can always keep that pen recorder in reserve, can't you," beamed Neil, massaging his shoulder. "Good man, I knew we could rely on you."

"And how do I smuggle it in then?" William wanted to know.

"Ah, there you are, Hettie," welcomed Neil, relieved as she made her presence known without the dress. "We were just talking about how to smuggle young William across the road in time for that meeting."

"I've been thinking about that," Hettie announced modestly. "And I think I've come up with the answer. I called in at the local chemist on the seafront yesterday and managed to borrow this sales kit from the cosmetics counter." She held it up for them to see.

Neil beamed. "Why, that's just what we want, isn't it, William? Don't you remember, we decided to distract that girl of yours with some free giveaways when she popped out for lunch leaving the door open, so you could sneak in behind her. She's bound to fall for it."

"How many times do I have to tell you – she isn't my girlfriend?" objected William heatedly.

"Of course not," interrupted Hettie soothingly. "Well, if that's all decided, I vote we go ahead. Where's Albert by the way – isn't he ready yet?"

"No," decided Neil firmly, "and he's not likely to be. I told him to keep his head down until after the meeting – one sight of him and Lady C would get all worked up about the shop again, and that's the last thing we need."

"Oh, what a shame - poor Bert. I suppose you're right." She sighed, hiding her disappointment. "In that case, we'd better get off then, if you're ready." She gave them both a quick inspection. "While we're at it, Neil – you'd better have another shave before the meeting, otherwise the ladies will be asking who the bearded lady is."

"Thanks for reminding me," said Neil, fingering his chin. "Don't wait for me – I'll be with you in two shakes."

Hettie consulted her watch. "You do that. Meanwhile, I think it's time we made a move, William, otherwise we'll miss her coming out. Come on dear, you wait by the door ready for me to give the signal. All set?"

"I suppose so," said William reluctantly.

* * *

Meanwhile, the atmosphere in Courtney Towers gave all the signs of building up into a grand opera. Sir Henry was pacing up and down in the marble hallway, every now and then turning to look up the staircase and consulting his watch.

"Come on, Margery, where the dickens are you? We'll be late for the meeting," he muttered peevishly to himself. "Ah, there you are," but it was Sally who appeared at the top of the steps, raising a finger to her lips before running down to join him.

"Ma's having trouble with her dress – she won't be long."

"Good Heavens, Sal, what's the hold-up? It's the Women's Forum, not Buckingham Palace."

"You don't understand, Dad. This isn't just any old meeting – they're going to elect her President – something she's been after ever since I can remember."

"Hmm. Well, at this rate, by the time we get there they'll probably have changed their minds."

Sally fixed her father with an imploring look. "Be patient, Dad. I thought this was part of the grand plan to make her more friendly to everyone, especially," her voice trembled, "the village shop and…"

"I know, love," he said hastily, patting her shoulder. "Hey, you'd better get changed, hadn't you? You don't want to be late as well?"

"Oh, Dad. I couldn't possibly go, I might meet up with you know."

"I don't think there's much danger of that, my dear," he let slip, remembering the hasty phone call he had received earlier on from Neil, warning him of what was about to happen.

Catching the inflection in his voice, Sally looked up quickly and was about to question him further when an arresting sight appeared at the top of the stairs.

"Oh, my word." Sir Henry's eyes widened to the size of golf balls. "What the devil?"

Remembering his earnest advice to dress simply and look suitably dignified for such an honoured occasion, Lady Courtney had taken him at his word and put on a dress that made her look not only dignified, but more... stately was the description that sprang to mind. In fact, the result of her countless changes had not only achieved the desired effect of riveting his attention and leaving him stunned, but reminded him of a barrage balloon his father had so vividly recalled seeing as a young man in the last war.

"How do I look?" She preened herself regally, opening a fan and waving it in a commanding fashion.

Open mouthed, Sir Henry was about to give vent to his feelings when Sally hurriedly dug him in the ribs, and he closed his eyes to shut out the sight, counted up to ten and mumbled feebly, "Good show, are we ready then?"

"Where's Lancelot?" his wife boomed suddenly. "Hasn't anyone told him this is a family occasion? The one event when I want him to be present, he disappears. I won't have him skulking off like this, the dratted boy. What will Edward think of us? Henry, do something, don't just stand there!"

"Yes, my love, just as you say." He was about to move off to do her bidding when Sally grabbed his arm suspiciously. "What was all that about the shop and William? Not that I care," she added defensively.

"Haven't got time to tell you about it now," he hedged. "Later, when this is all over – suffice it to say we'll have a deuce of a lot to be grateful to him for, if he manages to pull it off."

"But what do you mean, Dad? Pull what off? What's William doing then?" She looked after him with mounting alarm as he pressed the bell for the maid, and waited impatiently as the stately figure slowly descended the staircase.

* * *

Just at that moment, William wasn't quite sure himself. Poised as he was to dash across the street at a given notice, he was brought up short by the sight of a short dumpy figure appearing at the doorway opposite instead of the receptionist they were expecting.

"It's old Foxey," he croaked, forgetting where Hettie was – "what's he up to?"

"Don't know, luv," her voice was relayed back from her vantage point behind a curtain. "Ah, there's a truck arrived outside, and they're bringing a whole load of boxes out. Stay out of sight, looks as if they're loading up."

William was more than happy to comply. Anything to stave off the dreaded moment got his vote. The only drawback was that his nerves were rapidly reaching fever pitch.

"What are they doing now?"

"I'm trying to see." Then enlightenment came. "There's a sign on the truck saying, 'Stage Suppliers'. I know what that is, Neil told me. They're loading up some models of that development scheme of Fred's – it's for the village hall. And," her voice sharpened with excitement. "It looks as if old Foxey and Mavis are taking it there themselves!"

"Good, that gets rid of them for a bit." William heaved a sigh of relief. "And gives me a bit more breathing space," he said to himself.

His relief was short-lived. Almost immediately after the dust settled following the truck's departure, the door opened again, this time showing the flash of a dress as Sybil, the receptionist darted out.

"There she is," Hettie announced swiftly. "Now's your chance, Willie. Stand by while I catch her, and be ready to slip in."

The door banged, and William got up and patted his jacket to make sure the recording gear was still there, before taking up his position.

"Excuse me, madam, can I interest you in some free samples?" He heard Hettie's voice floating across the street, making the receptionist halt in her tracks. "What have I got?" her voice trilled. "You'd be surprised. Why don't you come and try out our latest brand of lipstick – it's just your shade. Why don't you see for yourself?" she coaxed.

William watched in admiration as he saw Hettie slowly manoeuvre the receptionist around so that her back was towards him. Seeing the coast was clear he made a quick dart across the street and slid in through the open door before he had time to think.

Flushed with her success, Hettie rushed back inside, elated at the way things had gone so far.

"Quick, Neil, he's in! Are you ready? It's time we were going."

"Hey, hang on, Het." Neil emerged from the back room, his face still covered with soap, a razor in his hand. "It's early yet, for Pete's sake."

"Don't forget we've still got to make sure Ed is ready and hasn't forgotten his talk," Hettie reminded him quickly. "You'd better put a shift on, and remember to call next door before we go. And don't forget to get that dress adjusted – you don't want to catch it in the door or something."

"Good thinking, Het," beamed Neil. "I'll do just that. Good thing we've got you on our side."

"Oh, go on with you," said Hettie pleased at the compliment, "you're as bad as Albert. Now, go and make sure Ed's ready and don't forget to shave, otherwise you'll get some funny looks from that young Veronica – she'll wonder what sort of family she's getting into."

But Ed Newman was already primed raring to be off, his notes clutched in his hand. The only thing he hadn't made plans for was what Veronica was going to do while he was giving his talk.

And from the noises overhead, it didn't seem if she was in any hurry.

"Vee, love, what are you doing up there? Don't you know we should be leaving right now?"

The noises stopped, and a stubborn head appeared around the corner of the stairs. "Gee, Pa, you don't want me along gumming up the works, do you?"

"Hey, I need you for moral support. How d'you think I'll feel faced with all those ladies peering up at me and giving me the old Bronx cheer like some sorta car salesman. Be human!"

"But Paw, what d'you want me to do - I've got nobody to sit with."

"What about young William, he'll be there, won't he?"

"Don't give me that, Paw, I've hardly seen a sign of him since he legged it across the garden – anyone would think I had the plague or summink."

"Oh." Then inspiration hit him. "What about Aunt Isobel? She'd be glad to sit with you – she's some mighty fine lady."

At the mention of the name, Veronica came down the last few steps and hissed. "Don't you know nuttin, Paw, it's a fella!"

Taken aback, Ed regarded her in bewilderment.

"What d'you mean? She strikes me as a fine upstanding lady."

"Exactly. She's got the muscles to go with it - I saw her knock you flying at the party."

"That's just her playful ways," he said uncertainly.

"Then why was she wearing garters at the party? She had socks on!"

"Well, um, I wouldn't know, Vee, perhaps she's got cold feet."

"Is that so? She's not the only one. I looked in just now to see if Willie was in, and that Aunt Isobel of yours was standing there in his vest and pants having a shave. Tie that in your billy can, Paw. That's one weird family, I kid you not."

A knock on the door saved Ed from answering. Tottering away to see who it was, he came face to face with Neil, carefully spruced up in a long flowing dress, beaming a welcome.

"Ah, there you are - all ready for the big event?"

Trying hard not to notice her heaving bosom, Ed gulped.

"Sure, good to see you, Aunt er...um. Everything gas and garters at this end... I mean gaiters," he corrected hastily, passing it off with a strangled laugh. "What I mean is everything is tiggerty boo, as you Brits would say, right?"

Neil laughed dutifully. "Got your talk all sorted then?"

"I sure have, ready when you are."

"Right, we'll be off then – would you like me to find a ringside seat for your charming daughter while you're busy with your presentation?"

"Why that's mighty handsome of you, Aunt...er."

"Isobel."

"Isobel, why of course. Isn't that great, Vee? Isobel will be able to put you right on everyone who's turning up, won't he...she?"

"In that case, perhaps she can tell us where that elusive nephew of hers is?" snapped Vee, unimpressed.

"Well, I can't tell you exactly where he is at the moment," answered Neil truthfully. "But I can tell you he's not very far away, and he will be joining us shortly with some splendid news – I hope," he added sotto voce.

Intrigued, despite herself, Veronica decided, "Well, in that case lead me to it, Auntie – you've got my vote. I sure would like to find out what that big palooka's up to right now."

Chapter Fourteen
Getting the Goat

If she'd had been able to put that question directly to William, he would have had to answer truthfully that he had no idea. Getting in to Foxey's inner den had been a relative walk over, due to Hettie's brilliant distraction, but trying to find somewhere to conceal himself once he was inside was proving quite a different matter.

He'd been prowling up and down the office for the best part of a quarter of an hour, tapping the walls, pulling away most of the furniture to see if there was anything hidden behind, until the place looked as if a cyclone had hit it, and still he was no closer to finding the secret panel Sir Henry had mentioned than the man in the moon. And the time seemed to be racing by.

Feeling tired and frustrated, William leaned wearily against the bookcase that covered the whole of one wall. It looked so solid he couldn't imagine anyone being able to get through it, even with the help of a battering ram. As he

258

rested his hand on a handy shelf to steady himself, he heard a click and a section of the bookcase suddenly gave way, and he found himself falling back into a void, and the floor came up to meet him.

Coming to slowly, he heard an exclamation the other side of the panel, and the murmur of raised voices in the room he'd just left.

"Come in gents, make yourself comfortable and we'll...my God, what's been going on here? Sybil! Where is that dratted girl? Sit yourselves down everyone, if you can find a chair, while I find out. Sybil! Oh, there you are. What the devil's the meaning of this? The place is an utter shambles. Have you let a mad dog in here, or something?"

The girl sounded equally astonished. "No sir, it wasn't me. I can't think what's happened!"

Plainly unsatisfied, Foxey could be heard prowling around, moving furniture. "Whatever it was, it couldn't have got in by itself. Well, I haven't got time to look now, I've got an important meeting. See that we are not disturbed, d'you hear?"

His voice dropped, and William strained to hear Foxey mutter. "Damn girl, can't trust anyone these days. Now to business, gents."

William felt around him anxiously. What did he do with the tape recorder? He felt in his pockets for the torch, with mounting panic. While he was doing so, he heard a voice that electrified him. Clive!

"Come on, don't let's waste time," a voice said peevishly.

He'd know that voice anywhere, after all the trouble he'd caused conning his way into Sally's family - what was he doing here? If only he could see what was going on. Then as his eyes grew accustomed to the dim light filtering through the cracks, he noticed a pinprick of light in the panel. Edging closer, he did his best to peer through the tiny opening and see what was happening. After a while, he could make out the back of a head, then as it shifted to one side, he caught sight of the planning man called Bernie Neil had been going on about, and in the background... he blinked at the shock... he saw the two tearaways who tried to rob the shop the other day.

"I totally concur," the bland voice of Bernie broke in smoothly – a voice that was used to getting his way on committees. "I take it we're all agreed on our course of action."

"Yea, man, cut us in on the action," piped up the one he remembered, called Jed.

"Now, wait a minute, all in good time," cautioned Foxey, living up to his nickname.

"There's something funny going on here – I just want to make sure we're private, and nobody can hear us."

William cursed inwardly. Here they were about to spill the beans and he didn't have any way of getting it down – he didn't even have a pencil – not that he could see anything. He began to move his foot around cautiously, but at Foxey's words he immediately froze. Everyone stopped speaking while Foxey moved around the room. He heard the door open suddenly, then close again.

"No, nobody's around," he heard Foxey announce. "Funny, I could have sworn…"

Whatever it was, he appeared satisfied. "Well now, let's get started."

Just at that moment, William moved his foot around exploring, and encountered something that made a sharp clang. He stopped and held his breath.

Immediately, Foxey broke off suspiciously, "Listen, what was that?"

"For Pete's sake, are we going to be here all afternoon?" complained Clive nervously. "I've got a business to run."

"Don't worry. I think you'll find this is worth waiting for," barked Foxey. "Something that'll make your car nicking sound like chicken feed."

Reaching out, William's hand closed over a slim object on the floor that he immediately recognised as Ed's prized secret weapon. Fat lot of good that was, he groaned, and as he reached out to stuff it in his pocket in disgust, a beam of tiny light shot out of the end of the pen and lit up a shape on the floor a few feet away. It was the tape recorder. His hopes rose at the sight of it, and he moved carefully inch by inch towards it and carefully picked it up, holding his breath and fumbling at the button, praying it would work. Feeling the fountain pen dig him in his pocket as he moved up to position the tape recorder, he fished it out and placed it for safety next to the tape recorder. Now all he could do was to wait and hope that the Women's Forum meeting didn't go on too long, otherwise Neil wouldn't be able to come to his rescue. As it was, it was beginning to get a bit stuffy in the confined space.

* * *

But the proceedings at the village hall involving the installation of a new president showed no signs of speeding up – if anything, it appeared to be continuing at a more leisurely pace than usual. Lady Courtney saw to that. As far as she was concerned, it promised to be the culmination of all her unfulfilled social ambitions, and she had no intention of missing one minute of it. When the results of the ballot were announced blandly by Aunt Ethel, taking upon herself to count the votes owing to the unexplained absence of the secretary, Lady Courtney seemed quite surprised and overcome at the unexpected honour, and proceeded to wave her fan in modest confusion.

Ignoring mutterings from the back of the hall, she allowed herself to be dragged to the platform, still protesting coyly. Once she had settled herself to her satisfaction, she signalled her family with a royal wave to join her at the table. In answer to cries of 'speech' from her supporters in the front row, she reluctantly drew out a prepared speech from her elaborate handbag that ran to six closely typed pages.

At first, she was listened to with a certain amount of good natured tolerance by the fair-minded section of the members, but after a while her droning voice created a certain restiveness, and the only spark of interest came from Veronica who leaned over to Neil and asked in a penetrating bored voice, "Say, who's that young guy sitting next to Lady C – the fish-face one with that piano wire stuck in his eye?"

Catching the blank look on Neil's face, Hettie leaned forward helpfully, "That's Lancelot, Lady Courtney's son – or rather, The Honourable Lancelot, I should say," she added with a touch of deference, "and that's his monocle I expect you were referring to."

"The Hon Lancelot? What's that when he's at home?"

Neil broke in bluntly, anxious to get things moving, and wondering how William was getting on at Foxey's. "That means he takes over when Sir Henry snuffs it."

Anxious to put the record straight in more acceptable terms, Hettie continued primly, "In the event of such an unfortunate occurrence, Lancelot would, I imagine, take on the title, as well as responsibility for the estate."

Having absorbed that information, Vee sat up with a jerk to ask the all important question. "Gee, is he married?"

"No," smiled Hettie. "At least, not as far as I know. It's no secret Lady Courtney would love to see him settle down with a suitable partner."

"You don't say," said Veronica with a speculative look in her eye, trying out the title to herself in a variety of ways with a dreamy look in her eyes, and evidently liking the sound of it.

She was so absorbed, she hardly heard Hettie lean forward and whisper excitedly, "your Dad is on next, Veronica."

Ed Newman was used to giving his talks to a mainly male audience, and was visibly put out when he looked out over a daunting sea of largely female faces. It didn't help much being faced with the unnerving sight of Aunt Isobel in the front row who was finding the wooden seats uncomfortable, and was fidgeting around so much that a section of her skirt seemed to be coming adrift.

"Hrm, gee, I would just like to say how honoured I am to be invited here today by your new President," he bowed to the gracious figure sitting next to him, "my old friend, Lady Courtney." His voice faltered as Neil hitched his dress up, revealing his hairy knees and his socks held up by a gaudy pair of garters underneath.

Aware of a scorching look from Lady Courtney, Neil hurriedly adjusted his dress, causing titters and nudging comments from nearby members.

His actions seemed to unnerve Ed Newman who started gabbling the first thoughts that came into his head. "I would like to start off showing some garters, I mean slides of some of our latest security devices that every household should have, to guard their legs. I mean, their homes." Wiping his forehead, he launched into his talk, gradually regaining his confidence until he ended up with the invitation to, "step right up during the interval and see for yourself how they work." Fingering his collar, he bowed to Lady Courtney and sat down again, getting his handkerchief out to mop his face.

Noting signs of muted hilarity in the front row, Lady Courtney frowned and banged the table with a gavel to command attention. "I am sure I speak for all of those present in thanking our special guest speaker, Mr Ed-ward Newman, for his fascinating and absorbing talk on 'security in the home', and above all for his extremely generous offer to become our sponsor, for which I am certain you will show your appreciation." She paused, allowing for the customary round of applause. "There will now be a short interval so you will all have the opportunity to examine the exhibits he has very kindly brought along. Refreshments are being served at the back of the Hall. Thank you."

"What a lovely talk. Wasn't that interesting what he was saying about?" enthused Hettie turning to Veronica, but Veronica was already making a beeline for the exit, following closely behind Sir Henry and his son, Lance, who were heading for the refreshment bar. "That's funny, I wonder where she's gone?"

But Neil was not interested. All he was concerned about was how young William was getting on. He was about to make his excuses and leave when he was buttonholed by Aunt Ethel who looked him up and down suspiciously. "And what was all that commotion going on at the beginning of the lecture? I saw those women giving you the once-over. I have you know this is a respectable establishment - no hanky panky here, if you please."

"No, of course not," he assured her quickly, trying to change the conversation. "The talk went off all right though, didn't it? You've got your sponsor?"

She faced him squarely like a sergeant major, tapping him on his chest. "Yes, I grant you that – let's hope he keeps to his promise." Giving him a final inspection, she gave a sharp intake of breath. "I said no hanky panky – I've heard all about you from Hettie, so kindly adjust your dress, if you please, young man. Your skirt's slipping again." And with that she stalked off.

Glancing around guiltily, Neil sat down and started to make some kind of temporary repair without much success, hoping nobody had seen him. He was still at it some ten minutes or so later when Lady Courtney bore down on him, beaming archly.

Smiling graciously, she insisted, "No, don't get up. I see our little talk has made a favourable impression on you. Now let me see, what newspaper do you represent? I'm sure I might be able to spare you a few minutes for an interview before the next session starts."

"I think you've made a mistake," began Neil desperately.

"Nonsense, you naughty young man – I've heard all about you sneaking in dressed up like that. What will you think up next – never mind, I forgive you. Now where shall we start? Of course, I can see the question trembling on your lips. You want to know exactly when I first became interested in this wonderful movement of ours - this noble sisterhood of suffragettes."

A gong clanged at the back of the hall signalling the end of the interval, and Lady Courtney reluctantly let go of his arm.

"Oh, bother, there goes the bell for the next session – never mind, I'll do my best to squeeze you in afterwards. Now don't go away," she added roguishly. "I shall keep my eye on you."

He was still rubbing his arm where her fingers had dug in when Hettie joined him.

"Gosh, you're keen, Neil. I saw you cornering Lady Courtney just now. I didn't realise you found it so interesting." In a burst of confidence, she admitted, "I must say she's turning out much better than I thought. She certainly knows how to handle people – perhaps she might even forget her old silly vendetta against the village, now she's President."

"I doubt it," sighed Neil, settling back as the seats started filling up again. "I bet it wouldn't need much to start her off again."

And it was not long before he was proved right.

His words were punctuated by the familiar sound of the gavel. Bringing the members to attention once again, Lady Courtney raised a hand. "Now I know you will not expect to hear anything more interesting than the fascinating talk we have just had - but I have a surprise for you. We were hoping to have in our midst an enterprising man with a pioneering vision, who has made it his life-long ambition to transform this little corner of England of ours into a Mecca for tourists. I am referring, of course, to that man of many parts – our own village saviour who is determined to put our village on the map, Mr Frederick Foxey."

As several people began muttering, she held up her hand. "Patience. I know you would like to hear all about this great scheme from the man himself, but as I understand he is unable to be with us today, his wife and staunch supporter, Mavis Foxey, has nobly stepped into the breach, and will explain it all to you - Mavis Foxey, ladies."

Swallowing, Mavis advanced nervously towards the microphone set up in front of a display board, and licked her lips. "Good afternoon, ladies. I am sorry my husband won't be here today to tell you all about his exciting new plans to develop our village." She smiled uncertainly.

"Of course, I can't promise to explain it as well as he could, as I don't suppose any of you will have heard about me."

A voice called out knowingly, "Oh, yes we have," and was immediately hushed.

"But I am sure you will know about my husband," she ploughed on, ignoring some of the ribald comments, and taking a quick look at her notes, "and of the sterling work he has done in promoting a programme of better homes for everybody."

"By bribery," someone hooted.

Ignoring the taunt, she smiled brightly, her face beginning to take on a defensive look.

Crash went the gavel, and Lady Courtney peered forbiddingly into the audience. "Quiet at the back there, or I'll have you ejected, whoever you are. Now, my dear, pray continue."

"Yes, well, if you look at the display my husband has prepared," she stepped to one side and pulled back a sheet revealing a model layout of a group of cottages, "you will see how carefully he has designed these holiday homes to blend in with the surroundings. They look like little gems, don't they?"

Noticing that some of the audience around him were beginning to nod off in the warmth of the sun slanting in through the windows, Neil decided it was time to ask some pertinent questions.

"Tell me," he asked sweetly. "Where is he proposing to build these, 'little gems'?"

Caught off guard, Mavis floundered for a moment, "Er, I believe most of them are planned to go along the seafront, and one or two others will be dotted about in a convenient position."

"Exactly where are these 'convenient positions'?"

Mavis consulted her map uncertainly. "I believe he mentioned just off the High Street - all comfortably furnished to the buyer's choice, of course," she added quickly.

"Can we see on the map where that is?" insisted Neil with a winning smile.

Hiding an instinctive refusal, Mavis reluctantly unfurled a map of the high street, showing dotted lines where the developments were planned.

"Thank you so much," purred Neil. "Dear me, don't say that dotted line means that you are doing away with all our well loved institutions - like the village shop, for instance?"

"Er, I'm sure that must be a mistake," allowed Mavis cautiously, "I would have to ask about that."

"And what about the cottage next door and the one after that - perhaps you could tell us who those are occupied by? Surely that belongs to Mr Newman, our new sponsor?"

In the middle of packing up his display items and relaxing over a drink in the background, Ed choked and spilled the contents, gasping, "Hey, what...what was that?"

"I understand that it is still in the preliminary stage," stuttered Mavis.

"You can't do away with our village shop," cried an outraged voice. "Where am I going to get my paper?"

"And groceries," piped up another.

"And my animals?" called out Hettie. "What's going to become of the new meat counter?"

"And what is that nice Mr Bridge going to do if the village shop closes?" joined in an elderly customer.

Coming to her rescue, Lady Courtney tried to calm their fears. "I am sure something will be found for him. In any case, it means we can start off with a fresh start without those nasty rumours flying about, eh Mrs Foxey?"

Reacting to the cue, Mavis responded with apparent reluctance, "Far be it for me to cast aspersions," she began.

"Go on, Mavis, you have our sympathy, under what must have been very trying circumstances," encouraged Lady C, her old resentments surfacing in her excitement. "Don't be afraid to speak out."

"They were and all," bridled Mavis. "I shan't be sorry to see him go, that's for sure, after what happened."

"Go on, tell us another one do," sang out a voice.

"It weren't no fairy tale!" burst out Mavis, stung by the taunt. "He hounded me round the shop, that's what he did. I'm a respectable woman, and don't put up with such behaviour, I never did!"

"What about the married lodger then?" jeered a voice.

"That's slander, and you know it!" shrilled Mavis, beginning to get rattled.

Thinking he'd push it along a bit, Neil stood up in mock horror. "How can you insinuate such things about this charming young lady – anyone would think she made a practice about knowing married gentlemen."

"Ho, and some," said a voice from the audience, some of whom were beginning to enjoy the unexpected entertainment.

"What about that Jim of yours, Sandra?" sang out someone knowingly from a different quarter. "He knew all about her, didn't he?"

A roar of laughter went up.

"And don't forget Arthur!"

"And what about Cyril - what price Cyril?"

A hunted look appeared on Mavis's face. She swung round to appeal to Lady Courtney. "I won't listen to any more of this – I'm going!"

Lady Courtney stood up, horrified. "Ladies! Restrain yourself. Let us have decorum at all costs. This is no way to behave – this is your President speaking. I beg you, remain calm and dignified. Remember who we are - we are the Women's Forum!"

At the sound of all the noise going on, a goat that had wandered in and was dozing happily at the back of the stage woke up, and feeling hungry started sniffing at a tasty looking drapery hanging in front of him.

Suddenly becoming aware of a strange munching noise coming from under her seat, Lady Courtney glanced down and screamed. Within seconds she lumbered onto her feet waving her arms, leaving a jagged portion of her dress in the goat's mouth. All around her, people started reacting, adding to the confusion, and the place was in an uproar. While this was going on, a cow poked her head through the curtains to see what all the fuss was about, and lifting its tail expressed its feelings on the subject to its satisfaction, causing a general exodus for the exit.

Taking a last look around the empty hall, Neil came to the conclusion there was nothing he could do to top that act, and feeling guilty about how William was managing, he wrapped his dress around him, and decided it was time he went to see how his nephew was getting on.

Chapter Fifteen
Panic Stations

William woke up with a jerk. He stretched himself and covered up a yawn, remembering just in time where he was. Jeepers, he panicked. What with the stuffy conditions, he must have dozed off. He pulled himself together and tried to think of what he might have missed. Looking around frantically, he was reassured that the recording light was still showing green, and the hum of conversation was continuing. Moving carefully to relieve his cramped position, he leaned across and listened.

"...so there we have it. Any questions?"

It was Foxey's voice, there was no mistake about that, but what he had been talking about was anyone's guess. Luckily, before he could gather his scattered thoughts together, it was Jed who provided the answer.

"What I'd like to know is, how did you manage to get planning permission for all those flaming houses," he wanted to know. "It must have cost a bomb in bribes?" There was a touch of envy in his voice, as if he would have been quite happy to have been involved.

"Hrm, never you mind," said Bernie blandly. "Let's just say I have a number of good friends in the right places."

"Blimey, I wouldn't mind being one of them – any chance of us joining this Council of yours?" His sally provoked a nervous burst of laughter. "Which reminds me, Mister, when do we get our cut, we're not in this for nothing, you know."

"Your turn will come, just shut it," said Foxey hastily, then another voice broke in, encouraged at the way the questions were leading.

"And where do I come in?"

"Right, Clive," said Foxey, sounding increasingly under pressure as the others gathered around to listen. "We'll need one of your cars if this idea of mine comes off – I take it you can get me some number plates to go with it?"

"Of course, but what's it all about?"

"Good, well that's all right," said Foxey choosing that moment to lean against the bookcase as a signal that the subject was closed.

His voice sounded so close that William jumped instinctively and bumped into the partition accidentally. He held his breath, waiting for the inevitable shout and discovery.

There was an immediate pause in the conversation and someone called out nervously. "What was that?"

"Nothing," was Foxey's irritable reply. "It's probably rats, the place is full of them."

"Now listen, you lot. This is only the beginning as far as I'm concerned. After I've cleaned up on this development, I've got something big planned that's just up your street if the conditions are right, so just wait your turn. You'll learn all about it in good time, okay?" His reply seemed to silence the hecklers, enabling him to continue. "Now, Bernie, you sure you've got the Council tied up on this? You've fixed it so we can go ahead?"

"Of course," was the smooth reply. "It's all passed, bar the shouting. It only needs a nod at the next meeting - we've got enough votes to carry it through. It's cost me enough," he admitted heavily. "Which reminds me, you promised me you'd pay me half down now and the rest when it goes through."

"Oh, yes," came the grudging reply. "Wait a minute, it's in the desk. Here you are," there was a rustle of notes. "Okay?"

There was another pause while William heard the notes being counted. "Yes," the voice sounded satisfied.

"Good, so that wraps it up. I think that's about it - a very successful afternoon, lads, if I may say so."

But he was wrong on both counts. As he spoke, a door slammed followed by anguished cries and a mad pattering of feet.

"Ruddy hell," Foxey swore. "What was that?"

The next minute William heard the door burst open and peering through a crack he had a ring-side seat and was able to see a dishevelled Mavis appear, clinging to the doorway for support.

"It's all gone wrong – you should have been there!" she cried.

"What happened?"

"They asked all sorts of questions. It wasn't my fault."

"What wasn't?" Foxey's face was a picture. "Didn't you use those notes I gave you explaining it all?"

"Yes, but they found out,"

"Found out – what?" shouted Foxey, losing his patience.

In a small voice, Mavis blurted out, "They know what's going to happen...about the shop."

"What?" his voice was almost drowned out by an immediate chorus of disbelief. "You didn't tell them?"

"They got it out of me – I didn't mean to, I swear it."

"Oh, my God!" groaned Foxey. "You half wit."

"What do we do now?" asked Bernie stupefied. "After all the trouble I've taken squaring those councillors – all for nothing. I can't believe it."

"Wait a minute," urged Foxey, seeking desperately for a way out, his mind still in shock at the thought of all the money he'd just paid out. "This needs thinking about – we've gotta keep calm whatever we do. Now listen, I don't pretend that this has not been a bit of a setback..." He paused to brood silently on the injustice of the situation, then mastering his emotions, he con-

282

tinued, "There's only one thing for it now - we go for the big one, Plan 'B'."

"It can't be any worse than Plan A," muttered Clive darkly.

"This is it," decided Foxey. "I was saving it for later, but we've got to keep one step ahead in this game. This is where you come in Jed, and you Smudge. You can handle the safe, while Clive arranges the getaway car. Right?"

Their faces brightened. "Now you're talking, what's the plan?"

"Gather around," Foxey glanced around to make sure nobody could hear. "This is how I see it." he broke off. "What's up, Mave?"

His wife seemed fascinated by something starting to slide up the bookcase wall behind their heads, and waved her hands at it dramatically.

"Look!" she breathed. "It's moving."

Foxey's head swung round impatiently. "Not now Mavis, we haven't got time to play silly devils."

"Blimey, she right," croaked Jed. "Look, it's there on the bookcase. Get it, Smudge!"

Obediently, Smudge made a dive and grabbed at a length of flex just as it was disappearing through a crack in the panelling. He clutched at the bookcase for support as he did so. "Got it!" he crowed triumphantly. "Blimey, what's that?"

There was a click, and to their amazement a section of the bookcase slowly began to swing open, revealing a startled William crouching there, desperately trying to haul in the other end of the cable connected to the recorder.

"Why, it's that damn shop boy again," cried Foxey aghast. "How did he get in there, and what's that, for gawd's sake?" He pointed with a shaking finger at the recorder box that William was trying to kick out of sight.

"Oh look, it lights up when you press this little button," said Mavis entranced, picking it up and trying it out.

There was a click, and they stiffened, electrified as Foxey's muffled voice was heard coming from the speaker, "...now, Bernie, you sure you've got the Council tied up on this? You've fixed it so we can go ahead?"

"Of course," was the smooth reply. "It's all passed bar the shouting. It only needs a nod at the next meeting - we've got enough votes to carry it through. It's cost me enough. Which reminds me, you promised you'd pay me half down now."

"Turn it off!" shouted Bernie, losing his composure and turning pale. "Turn the thing off – this'll ruin me if it gets out!"

"Don't worry," said Foxey grimly. "I'll see to that. Deal with it, Jed."

"Like this?" His henchman drove his heavily studded boot through the wooden housing, flattening it out of shape.

William shuddered and all his hopes curled up and died at the sight.

"Now, where's your proof?" snarled Foxey, peering down at him, smirking with satisfaction. "So you thought you'd get the better of me, did you?" He clenched his fists. "Better men than you have tried, and a fat lot of good it did them. We'll deal with you later, sonny boy…"

He was interrupted by Jed who was advancing into the recess and flashing his torch around. "Here, listen, that's queer, you guys. Why, it looks like some sort of a trapdoor at the back. Someone give us a hand, I can just about lift it up…ugh…that's done it. Blimey, I can feel a bit of a draught coming through. D'you think it's some sort of a tunnel, Boss? Look, there's some steps going down. I wonder where it goes?" Behind him, Smudge kicked something on the floor, and picking it up absently popped the fountain pen recorder in his pocket as a keepsake, in front of William's horrified gaze.

Casting an indifferent glance at what they were doing, Foxey climbed in and peered through the opening with some reluctance. "Here, let me see." He glanced down uncertainly into the murky depths and shivered. "We'll take a decko at that first thing in the morning when we we've got more time," he decided, his mind still grappling with the more immediate problem of how the devil he was going to get the money back he'd so lavishly showered on Bernie.

But time was already running out on them. At that moment, a police siren could be heard in the distance getting louder and coming closer, and the next minute a car screeched to a halt outside with a slam of brakes, followed by an authoritative thump on the front door. It was in fact, Police Constable Cuthbert responding to a tip-off about the animals running riot at the hall, but they were not to know that.

"It's the rozzers," panicked Jed. "What'll we do?"

"They mustn't find me here!" bleated Bernie.

"Nor me," one of the others echoed wildly, looking hopefully at Foxey for a signal.

The timely interruption presented William with a sudden inspiration. "I told them I was coming here," he shouted, hoping someone outside would hear – "he's got a warrant."

What they thought Constable Cuthbert was proposing to do with the warrant they neither knew, nor cared. But it was enough to set Foxey off in a furious rage, and he advanced on William, his eyes smouldering. "Wait till I get my hands on you."

"Let's get out of here," someone yelled and there was a concerted rush for the bookcase, trampling over William in a mad scramble, resulting in a mass of jostling bodies getting jammed together in the narrow opening in their frantic rush to escape.

"Just a minute, don't panic!" screamed Foxey, rapidly losing his cool, grabbing hold of Jed as he passed. He pointed at William on the floor. "Get Smudge to help you tie him up, while I get a gun. We can't leave him behind – he knows too much."

Scrabbling through the desk, he quickly pounced on a pistol in one of the drawers and hurriedly followed on after the others.

Peering nervously down the tunnel, he yelled, "Wait for me," and promptly lost his footing and plunged down the crumbling stairway with a muffled howl.

Hearing him cursing in the background, the others came to a ragged halt while they waited for him to catch up. As they forged ahead in a straggly line, William did his best to keep up despite having his hands tied behind his back, trying to figure out where the tunnel was likely to come out, and how he could get away.

After a few minutes the tunnel began to level out, and snatches of conversations broke out around him, "Hold the torch steady someone, I can't see where I'm going...you've just trodden on my foot, you clumsy idiot...hurry up in front." And the petulant voice of Bernie complaining in the background, "I'm late for a meeting. I say, you fellows, let me through." Then some-one noticed the difference in the uneven path-way underfoot and gasped thankfully, "Look, the ground's rising again."

Finally, the ones in front came to a sudden stop and the others caught up and began to col-lide with each other. "Mind out where you're go-ing."

Then a perspiring figure pushed through to the front, revealing a bedraggled Foxey.

"Where's the torch?" he complained, looking weary and puffing from the unexpected effort in-volved. He looked at his watch. "That's five min-utes I make it. We've been going in a straight line so we must be somewhere across the road at this rate, if I'm not very much mistaken – probably in one of the back gardens. Now who's going up to have a look?"

He glanced around for a likely volunteer, and settled on Jed. "You're a strong lad, see if you can find a way out – no point in everyone having a go. We'll wait here," he ordered, deciding to place himself at the foot of the stairs in the hope that he would be able to frisk Bernie as he came past, and relieve him of some of his cash that he considered was gained under false pretences.

After a few minutes, some of the group started growing restive and Foxey called up,

"Hurry up, Jed, what's happening?"

There was a pause, then an excited voice shouted down, "Jeepers, you'll never guess where we are – come and look!"

Reluctantly giving up the idea of getting his money back for the time being, Foxey scrambled up the last stretch of tunnel to see what all the fuss was about, motioning the others to follow.

Prodded by Smudge, William managed to elbow his way up somehow and finally made it to the bottom of a short flight of stairs, and after mounting the last few steps found to his amazement they had ended up inside Ed's fortified shed.

"Blimey, where are we?" Smudge goggled at all the hardware spread around, piled up on the shelves.

Enlightenment came to Foxey. "Here, I know where this is. I've been here before - it's where Ed Newman keeps all his security stuff." He glanced around sarcastically. "Anyone want to lock up their valuables?"

There was a hoot of derisive laughter. "Do you mind," growled Jed, "I'd be the laughing stock of Dartmoor if they caught me owning any of this lot. Let's get out of here before the rozzers find us."

"I have mentioned it before, but I do have an important appointment," argued Bernie plaintively."

Foxey eyed the other's bulging pockets sourly. "It's all very well for some…" his voice died away as he glanced around furtively. "That reminds me, I seem to remember Newman had a safe knocking about somewhere. I wonder where he's hidden it?"

Jed noticed William edging around in front of a curtained recess, and his voice grew shrill.

"Watch 'im, Smudge, he knows something."

Smudge made a lunge and knocked William sideways. Unable to save himself with his hands tied, he fell awkwardly, hitting his head on the corner of the staging and slumping on the floor.

"You haven't hurt him, have you?" asked Bernie nervously, taking a step backwards towards the door.

"No, fat chance," voiced Clive bending forward to take a closer look. "Take more than that to finish him off. He's just knocked out for a while." Straightening up, he added his voice to the protest. "But Bernie's right, I think we ought to be shifting. Word soon gets around, and we don't want to be stuck here when the police turn up." He licked his lips. "How do we get out of here?"

"Wait a minute," ordered Foxey, his eyes gleaming. "I think I've got something here that might interest you, gents – something that might make your time here worthwhile." He bent forward and pulled the curtain aside with a flourish, causing several gasps.

"Blimey! He's right," murmured Smudge awed. "What d'you think of that, Jed – can you bust it?"

Jed snorted, "Hand me a tin opener. No," he added contemptuously, rolling up his sleeves, "it's like stealing money from a kid's money box. I'll just breathe on it."

"Is there anything in it, boss?" asked Smudge eagerly.

"He's got a pile of money in there from all my orders, for a start," said Foxey moodily, thinking bitterly of all his ambitious plans gone in smoke. "Don't waste time, let's bust it open and see what's inside."

To William, who was just beginning to surface groggily, their concerted move towards the safe set off warning bells in his mind, and acted as a bugle cry for action. Remembering Ed's glowing description of his patent burglar alarm, he cautiously moved his foot sideways until it nudged the button. He had no need to worry about anyone noticing. All eyes were focussed intently on what Jed was doing as he manipulated the tumblers on the safe. Taking a deep breath, William lifted his heel and brought it down with as much force as he could muster on the button, and their ears were blasted by a vicious outbreak of barking, so hideous it sounded as if all the hounds of hell had been let loose.

Held paralysed for a split second by the terrifying ordeal, someone screamed and there was an immediate stampede for the exit, trampling over William and knocking him senseless for the second time that afternoon. In the rush, nobody noticed that the doors opened quite easily from the inside, but even a thousand locks in place would not have prevented them from getting out, such was the momentum of their flight. In passing, Smudge collided with Jed, and something dropped from his pocket and rolled on the floor.

Chapter Sixteen
Hands Off

William woke up gradually, conscious of the daylight streaming in through the windows and of a nurse bending over him. He turned his head away from the sudden brightness and closed his eyes. When he opened them again, the beaming face of his Uncle Neil swam into view.

"Where's your dress, Auntie?" he murmured drowsily.

"Don't need it any more, do I?"

"Why, has Constable Cuthbert made an honest woman of you?" William hazarded a fatuous guess.

"Nah, it's all thanks to you, my lad."

"Me?" said William bitterly. "You're having me on. I'm afraid all my efforts were a wash-out. They destroyed all the evidence."

"Not all the evidence," his uncle stressed, with a note of triumph in his voice. "Don't forget that recorder of yours."

"But…but I couldn't make it work – it was absolutely useless." He gripped the bedclothes in frustration, full of remorse for letting the side down.

"Useless, is it? We'll see about that. Nurse!" Neil caught the eye of a passing member of staff.

"Yes, sir?" The young nurse eyed him politely, but seemed more interested in William, giving him an extra special smile.

"Can you pull the screen across – we need a bit of privacy."

"I really should ask Sister, sir, but seeing as it's Master William I think we might allow it, just this once." And with a swish of the curtain, she ran the screen around them, and gave another perky grin before disappearing.

"What was all that about?" William stared after her mystified.

"You don't suppose they're talking about anything else at the moment, do you? You've put the town on the map overnight with your exploits."

"What are you talking about?"

"Just this," grinned Neil, deciding to put his nephew out of his misery. With a flourish he brought out of his pocket the missing fountain pen recorder.

At the sight of it William gaped. "But I thought Smudge walked off with that. How did you get hold of it?"

"He must have dropped it, and it's a good job he did," enthused Neil. "Get a load of this." So saying, he flipped a switch on the side of the pen and pointed it at the screen in front of them.

Hearing the familiar voice begin, accompanied by the back view of Bernie appearing on the screen, William caught his breath. "It worked after all. I can't believe it!"

"Nor did I, when I saw it," confessed Neil, "and you ought to have seen Ed's face when I showed it to him. He nearly went berserk."

Questions began to pour out of William. "Did they get the safe open? Does that mean he's lost everything? He'll be going back to the States after all that, I suppose." He felt an overwhelming sympathy for Ed, tempered by the thought that he wouldn't be hounded by Veronica any more.

"Not exactly, he'll tell you," Neil said mysteriously. "That's for him to decide. All I know is that I've got the evidence I need to clear myself, and make sure that Bernie character gets his desserts." He heaved himself off the bed. "I fear this is where I must say good-bye, young William. You've saved my bacon, for which I'll be eternally grateful – and I know your uncle Albert will feel the same. Now I must leave you and make way for all the rest of the family who are waiting to congratulate you. I know there's a certain young lady outside who's dying to see you." He grinned, "I made sure I got in first."

"You don't mean…?" William's face lit up, unable to believe it could be true.

Neil smiled understandingly, and slapped him on the back before leaving with a farewell salute. "Got it in one – good luck!"

William sat there hugging himself with anticipation. The next minute the screen was thrust aside, and to his horror the eager face of Sybil the receptionist appeared, wiping the silly grin from his face. Casting a quick look around to see they were alone, she launched herself at William before he had a chance to avoid her advances.

"Oh, Mr Bridge, William, how can I thank you." The rest of her words got lost as she decided to demonstrate how she felt by flinging her arms around his neck and fastening her lips on his.

Coming up for air, William pulled himself free. "What –what's all this in aid of?"

It was exactly the same question Sally was asking herself as she tripped in a few moments later only to see William's lipstick coated face coming up for the third time as he tried to free himself.

"Oh!" Sally's face froze. She rapped on the metal bed frame. "This is becoming a habit." Her voice started to tremble, "I came here ready welcome the hero home and forgive everything but it seems I'm not the only one. How could you!"

"But…but I don't know how it happened."

"I would have thought that was pretty obvious. Goodbye." She broke of furiously, turned on her heel and stormed out.

"Now look what you've done." William dabbed at his face unsuccessfully.

"What was she steamed up about?" Sybil looked surprised. "I only came to thank you."

"I think she got the message," groaned William, wondering what he had done to deserve this latest calamity, "but why?"

"Oh, I'm sorry," said Sybil innocently, getting out her compact and repairing the damage, oblivious of the havoc she had caused. "Didn't I say? Well, now that horrid man Foxey has done a bunk, my boyfriend has stopped being jealous and has asked me to marry him – and I've got you to thank for it all. He's so afraid of losing me again we're getting married by special licence tomorrow –isn't that great?"

"Great," repeated William mechanically. "How does that leave me?"

"Oh, golly, I see what you mean. I am sorry. Look, don't move, I'll see if I can catch her and explain. Don't go away."

Wrapped in the depths of despair William closed his eyes sunk into gloom. Feeling at his lowest ebb he was convinced that whatever else befell him, nothing could possibly happen now to make the situation any worse. But he was wrong.

Suddenly there was a commotion in the corridor outside, and shouts could be heard. Doors were being slammed, followed by the sound of running feet and the next moment the door crashed open. Opening his eyes, William was confronted by a frenzied figure swaying unsteadily in the doorway, before he pulled off his scarf to reveal the familiar face of Foxey. Taking a swig from a bottle to steady his nerves, he fumbled in his pocket and produced a gun, at the sight of which William instinctively dived under the bedclothes.

"I swore I'd get you, you meddlesome young swine!" cried Foxey, swinging around wildly, trying to focus his bleary eyes on his target. Hearing renewed shouts from outside, he lost his head and pressed the trigger in a panic. Instead of a fuselage of shots, however, all he achieved was a series of clicks. With an oath, he threw the gun down. "That's another dud that blasted Yank sold me! You haven't heard the last of this from me!" And with that he stumbled out of the room, the sound of his departure growing fainter as he careered down the corridor.

Alarmed at the disturbance, Sally ran down the hospital corridor at a speed she would have been shocked to see in her students, and arrived panting at the door of the ward that she had stormed out of a short while ago. Catching a glimpse of Foxey vanishing around the bend, and seeing the gun on the floor, she flung herself into the room fearing the worst.

"Oh darling," she wailed, wrapping her arms around the lump in the bedclothes, fearful of what she might find. "I love you. Sybil's told me everything. Tell me I'm not too late."

The next moment, the lump stirred and a tousled head appeared. Wondering whether he was dreaming, William shook his head to try to clear his scattered senses, and caught hold of her to make sure she was real.

Gazing down at him tenderly, Sally reassured him. "Yes, it's me, Sally, and I'll never disbelieve you ever again. Oh darling, say you'll forgive me."

In a daze, William pulled her close and kissed her, half afraid she might change her mind and vanish again as a figment of his imagination. "Of course." He looked at her earnestly. "You're sure you mean it this time – I'm not dreaming?"

There was a discreet tap on the door and a nurse appeared. "Are you all right, Mr Bridge?"

Anxious that his lovefest with Sally would not be disturbed, he hastily told her everything was fine.

Reassured, the nurse confided, "I'm so glad. There's been some nut case." She giggled and amended it to, "I should have said, some poor man – they say he's not quite right in his head – who's been running amok around the wards frightening everyone. I hope he didn't disturb you?" Her eye fell on the gun and glanced reproachfully at Sally. "Visitors aren't allowed to bring toys and suchlike into the wards, you know, Miss." Then, conscious of Sister's iron discipline and nervous she might be losing marks on her performance, she hurried on, "I really ought to report it, but seeing as how he didn't worry you, I'll see to it myself." Picking up the gun she tucked it into her waistband, and making sure the coast was clear she hurried off to dispose of it downstairs.

"Now, Willie, precious," ordered Sally firmly, settling him down more comfortably with a pillow behind his head, "tell me what's been happening. I want to hear all about it, and what was all that commotion going on before I got here?"

Gathering his thoughts together, William embarked on what had happened since he last saw her, leaving out the bits he felt would best be left unsaid.

"Golly, what will Ma say when she hears her precious dealer is nothing but a fraud?" she laughed gleefully when his story came to an end.

"I don't know," William admitted candidly. "But let's face it, she won't be exactly tickled pink about it – especially when she finds out I was the one who sussed him out."

"I see what you mean." Sally bit her lip. "She doesn't usually like to admit she's made a mistake. Oh, Willie love, what are we going to do?"

At that point their immediate problem was shelved with the re-appearance of the nurse poking her head around the corner of the door. "Excuse me sir, you've got some more visitors – your uncle, Mr Bridge, and a friend."

"How are you, my boy?" asked Albert bustling in, closely followed by Hettie, eager to find out how he was.

Taking the view there was no time like the present for announcing his glad news, William glanced up for confirmation at Sally who nodded and gave him a hug. "We…that is, Sally and I," he gulped, "are going to get married."

Beaming benevolently, Albert looked in wonder at Sally. "Is this true, Miss Sally?"

Laughing, Sally, corrected him. "Well he hasn't
actually got down on his knees and proposed –
but yes, he's got it right, at last, and less of the
Miss Sally, if you please. All my friends call me
Sally, so you'll have to get used to it, I'm afraid."

"Oh, luv, I'm so pleased for both of you," Hettie
said impulsively. She looked up coyly at Albert.
"Shall we tell them our news now?"

Albert huffed and puffed. "Well, it's like
this..."

Bursting with excitement, Hettie decided she
couldn't wait any longer and held up her hand
triumphantly, showing off a ring. "We're going
to get married as well - look, we're engaged!"

"Oh, I'm so glad!" cried Sally. "That makes two
of us."

William gazed up at his uncle, impressed.
"Congratulations!" and, enlightened, turned to
Hettie. "So that's who you were talking about."

"Yes, he got round to it at last." She smiled contentedly.

"Hrm." Albert looked embarrassed. "It wasn't
because I didn't want to. It's just that I couldn't

ask her until I was sure everything was going to turn out all right, you see."

"So what decided you?" William, puzzled, looked at each of them in turn.

Albert coughed. "Well, it turned out that Edward, or Ed, as he likes to be called, was so overjoyed you rumbled that Foxey character and stopped them raiding his safe, he wants to show his appreciation."

"You'll never guess!" squealed Hettie, unable to contain herself any longer. "He wants to put some money into the shop, and he's even forking out for temporary staff while we go off on our honeymoon!"

"I can't believe it!" whistled William, relieved and happy at the way things had turned out for both of them. "That's very generous – very generous," he repeated thoughtfully, wondering how it would affect his standing with Veronica.

Looking bashful, Albert said, "We thought we'd have a quiet wedding at Hettie's village just down on the coast. No fuss, Hettie doesn't have any close family left, so we thought we'd make it just the two of us – hope you don't mind."

"Of course we don't, do we Willie?" Sally flung her arms around Albert.

"No, no. It's the best thing that could happen. We're delighted for both of you."

"There's just one thing." Albert hesitated. "I said you'd keep an eye on things at the shop, just while we're away. I hope you don't mind, that is, if you are feeling fit enough, my boy – how long do you think they will keep you here?"

Sally cast an anxious glance at William to see his reaction after all he'd been through, but William hastened to reassure him. "I feel fine, Uncle, don't worry about me. I can leave as soon as they let me."

As if to settle the argument the door swung open, and Sister swept in followed in her wake by an apologetic nurse.

"In view of the highly irregular happenings taking place in my Ward, I suggest that would be the wisest move for all concerned, Mr Bridge," she announced in a tone of voice that brooked no argument. "Since the patient seems to be in a perfectly fit condition, nurse, you will kindly gather Mr Bridge's effects together and see that he leaves immediately."

"I say," protested Albert, "that seems a bit high-handed, what?"

Sister snorted. "I am not in the habit of allowing drunks to run amok in my Ward using threatening behaviour, and on top of that hearing reports one of my own staff has been involved - it is not the kind of behaviour I have come to expect, or tolerate."

Catching sight of the nurse looking on anxiously in the background, William intervened hastily. "I'm sure she was trying to be helpful – we're most grateful for all she has done."

"That's as may be," judged the Ward Sister, slightly mollified. "In that case, I will say no more other than to inform you that you have my permission to leave, and you can return to your duties, Nurse."

With a final acknowledgement to William's visitors she nodded at the Nurse who cast a grateful glance at William before leaving.

"Oh, that reminds me." Sister paused as she was about to follow. "I suppose you don't know anything about this?" She held up a card for them to see. Across the front was scrawled the message, "Hands off – he's mine!"

Sally glanced at William and tried not to giggle.

"No, Sister, it wasn't me," intervened William truthfully.

"I thought as much," commented Sister drily, and tucking it under her arm swept out.

"Whew! I think that does it. Come on Sally, the sooner we get out of here the better," decided William.

"And I think it's time we went and let you sort yourselves out, my boy," agreed Albert hurriedly. "So glad you're feeling better." He patted William on his shoulder. "We'll leave the shop in your good hands." Kissing Sally, he congratulated her warmly, "Delighted at the news Miss Sally, I mean, Sally - absolutely delighted. Glad to hear he's got someone to look after him at last." Turning absently on discovering Hettie waiting behind him patiently he said, "Oh yes, come, my dear, we must be off. Important things to do, eh?"

Giving a half despairing glance at William and Sally, Hettie reminded him, "Don't forget the money and the key."

"Ah, to be sure," Albert started apologetically. "Almost forgot. Here's some money to go on with, oh, and the shop key. You won't be able to get in without it, eh? Ha-ha."

"Get on with you, luv," nudged Hettie lovingly. "We're keeping the taxi driver waiting. Bye all!"

Chapter Seventeen
A Case of Mistaken Identity

If Sally imagined the removal of Fred Foxey from the scene would have weakened her stepmother's opposition to William and the shop she was sadly mistaken. Humiliated by her recent experiences at the village hall, Lady Courtney was even more resolved to squash any talk of marriage. In fact, the mere mention of the possibility sent her into a violent rage.

So when Sally raised the matter with her father next morning expecting his blessing, a hunted look came into his face and he hurried drew her into his study and shut the door, after carefully looking up and down the corridor, before he was satisfied they were alone.

He sat her in a chair and collapsed at his desk mopping his face, and it was some minutes, after his fingers stopped twitching, and he was able to manage a strained smile, before he could bring himself to answer her.

After gulping several times he croaked, "You know if it was up to me, I'd give you my blessing like a shot, but," his fingers started twitching again, "you don't understand what it's been like these past few days since that meeting – what I've had to put up with."

He searched in his mind for an apt description to explain his feelings. "She's been raging round the place like a mad bull. Wait, that doesn't sound right," he reflected. "A mad cow? No, I think I was right the first time." He looked at her earnestly, "Can't you give her at least a chance to calm down?"

"But Dad, how long do I have to wait?"

"A year or so?" he tried hopefully.

"A year or so?" she cried indignantly, causing the desk light to wobble. "You're joking! You are, aren't you?" she pleaded.

"Hush," he begged hastily, "she might hear." Seeing her eyes flash in open rebellion, he added anxiously, "If there were only some way we could get around it." He looked at her hopefully for inspiration.

"Well," she said slowly, "we were thinking of doing it all low key, without any fuss or attention."

"Yes, yes. How?" He grasped at the lifeline like a drowned man.

"Why, by special licence, of course," she said brightly. "Just one or two close friends as witnesses, then before you know what's happened, it's all over, cut and dried. And by the time we get back from our honeymoon, she'll have forgotten all about it."

He shuddered. "I hardly think that's likely."

"Well, we're going to, whether she likes it or not," she decided firmly, getting up. "That's definite, sorry Dad."

"Well, I wish you luck," he said doubtfully. "I'd dearly love to be there, you know that, but in the circumstances I don't think that's a very good idea."

"I know." She smiled sympathetically. "Wish me luck."

He gave her a hug. "All the luck in the world, my love – you're the best of the bunch. Let me know how you're getting on, and don't forget," he whispered conspiratorially, "send all the bills to me in a plain envelope."

As he waved her off, he prayed to himself nervously, "Let's hope Margery doesn't hear about it, otherwise all hell will be let loose." As he tried to shut his mind to the full horror of the spectacle a door closed quietly down the corridor.

True to his word, William turned up at the village shop the next morning to see what he could do. Knowing it was Sunday, he decided not to hurry and by the time he got there all the papers had been sold, and having taken over from a young lad in charge who was grateful at being relieved, he sat down and gave himself up to loving thoughts about Sally.

After a while, the emptiness of the shop and the insistent ticking of the clock began to intrude, and he thought perhaps he'd better read the notes Albert had left behind, in the hope they would suggest something useful for him to do to relieve the monotony. Under the heading, 'Important', the first item left him quivering nervously, reminding him to call on Ed next door and deliver his regular weekend order without fail.

The alarming suggestion happened to coincide with the tinkling of the bell, and he went into an immediate panic fearing the caller might be Veronica. At the sight of a young man entering the shop his gangling nerves subsided, and he half rose asking if he could help.

The young man seemed equally nervous. "No, no, just browsing, if that's all right?"

"Of course, go ahead." Relieved, William went back to examining his list, carefully circling the first item and transferring it to the end of the queue. The other items were fairly straightforward and boiled down to keeping an eye on things, and making sure everything looked reasonably tidy. That was the easy part, he concluded, deciding to shelve the order for Ed until later, after Sally had been and brought him up to date with the latest news.

His eyes strayed to the clock wondering what was keeping her, and every now and then he glanced at the young man to check what he was doing. Seeing him move along the shelves picking up magazines at random, William came to the conclusion that he was using the excuse to browse while he was waiting to meet someone.

Becoming bored, the young man caught sight of something on the bottom shelf out of sight, and dragging up a chair sat down to read it, chuckling every now and then as he did so. Thinking him harmless, William dismissed him from his thoughts and returned to thinking of Sally, and was just about to get in touch with her when the telephone rang and he sprang to answer it.

"Willie?" Sally voice wailed, "Ma's on the warpath!"

William gulped. "What's happened?"

"She must have heard me telling Dad about us getting married, and she's on her way over to see you. She's hopping mad."

"She is?" He looked around apprehensively, expecting the door to crash open at any minute.

"Sorry I couldn't let you know earlier, darling," Sally was contrite. "If you leave now we could meet up somewhere."

William lowered his voice. "I can't, there's someone in the shop – I don't know who it is."

Sally's anguished squawks came floating over the line. "Blow the shop – it's our whole future at stake! I know her – she'll, she'll ruin everything!"

He fought down his fears. "I can't leave now, I promised uncle I'd look after things. Besides," his common sense took over, "she can't create a scene in front of strangers."

"Well, promise me you won't do anything silly, love – don't argue with her, that'll only make her worse."

"I promise."

"Right, I'll be right over to back you up – I'll see if I can get Dad to give me a lift."

William replaced the receiver thoughtfully. Things seemed to be hotting up, and he was not quite sure what the outcome would be. What was needed, he decided, was some sort of minor miracle.

As if in answer to his prayers, the shop bell tinkled and in wandered Ed Newman.

"Hi, Willie," he beamed. "How'ya feeling?" Catching sight of the stranger, he fingered his collar slightly embarrassed, looking from one to the other. "Gee, I see you've already got to know each other."

"Er, no," began William, seeking enlighten-ment.

The young man seemed apologetic. "I was just browsing, while I was waiting for…"

Ed Newman broke in hastily. "Don't tell me, she's always late. You can bet your bottom dollar on that." He turned to William, sensing he was treading on the edge of a volcano. "See here, Willie, a lot has happened since you got tied up with that Foxey character across the way. Yes sir, a lot has happened." Placing an arm around William, he massaged it affectionately. "I don't know how to put this son, but you've got to try to understand how a girl's mind works. Take Veronica, for instance."

At the mention of her name, William jumped and glanced around with a hunted expression. "She's not here?"

"Gee, that's what I'm trying to tell you, Willie. See here, I know how you feel about her, and I'm mighty sorry at the way things have turned out. It's just that she's decided it's time to move on."

An expression of rising hope lit up his face. "You're going back to the States?"

"No gee, we'll be around a long time let, if you good people will have us."

He laughed, highly amused in a way that dashed William's last remaining hopes.

"No, sirree, I see a big enterprise opening up this side of the pond. What I'm trying to tell you Willie, is that while you were stuck in that hell hole, Vee came along to hear my talk at your village hall, and made the acquaintance of our friend here and they got on so well together that, gee, I don't know how to put this. I know you're going to take this on the chin like I just knew you would." He moistened his lips and appealed to the young man who had standing by, hopping from one foot to the other.

Nerving himself up to the challenge, the young man shut his eyes and explained in a rush, "I asked Veronica to marry me, and she's accepted. Sorry, and all that."

"You've – what?" exclaimed William dizzily, unable to take it in.

"I say, it's all above board, and all that tommy rot. I did ask Mr Newman's permission first."

Ed winced at the revelation, and mastered a smile.

"Gee, I hope you won't think too badly about it, Willie. You know what Vee is like when she makes up her mind."

"Mind?" uttered William feebly. "Why that's," he searched for an appropriate word, without trying to sound too overjoyed in the circumstances, "just unbelievable."

Overcome by an enormous feeling of relief, he rushed forward to show his gratitude, causing the young man to jump back, instinctively fearing a sudden assault.

Seizing his hand, William pumped it up and down. "My hearty congratulations, old boy. Sorry, I don't know your name."

Mopping his forehead, Ed was all apologies. "Say, I thought you knew it was Sally's brother, Lance."

"Sally's brother?" All at once, the humour of the situation struck him and he began to laugh feebly.

Bursting into the shop minutes later, Lady Courtney took one look at the spectacle of the three of them slapping each other on the back, and jumped to the conclusion that they were congratulating William on his marriage plans.

Heaving with indignation, she pointed her umbrella and cried dramatically, "I forbid this marriage!"

In the stunned silence that followed Lance tried to grab her arm to restrain her, but she brushed him aside. "Don't bother me now, wretched boy. Out of my way!"

"But Margery, we thought you'd be pleased," attempted Ed bewildered. "He's a splendid young man – we're all proud of him."

"Oh, Ed-ward, you don't understand. The humiliation of it all - to think our family would come to this!"

Not known for being easily rattled, Ed was offended. "I'll have you know, Margery, we may not be high society but we come from good honest stock, the backbone of our great country."

"Don't confuse me, Ed-ward, this is a family matter." She glanced around angrily. "Oh, I can see I'm just wasting my time arguing about it here. I'll have it out with the boy's aunt – she'll see the whole idea's utterly ridiculous!" And with that she stormed out of the shop.

"What the heck's she talking about?" Ed asked the others. "Do you know?"

"Search me, I don't have an aunt," replied Lance with feeling.

"Do you, Willie?"

But William could only shake his head, trying to work out what sort of reception their visitor would receive at the hands of his formidable aunt.

Chapter Eighteen
Equal Rights

Had she known better, Lady Courtney would not have chosen Sunday morning as the best day to have it out with Aunt Ethel. For it was the one morning after early morning church service that she felt uplifted enough to thoroughly clean out the kitchen and downstairs with a pure and righteous heart, before putting her feet up for a well earned rest after lunch.

At the insistent sound of knocking on the front door she put down her dish cloth and straightened her apron, before reluctantly answering the summons.

"Drat it, whoever it is," she muttered to herself, opening the door. "Yes?" she said impatiently, then recognising the caller. "Oh, it's you, Lady Courtney. Come in, the place is in a bit of a mess. I'm just tidying up."

"Really, I get my staff to look after that sort of thing."

"Maybe," sniffed Aunt Ethel. "Well, we're not all that lucky, are we?" Aware her visitor was giving the room a somewhat disdainful glance, she said brusquely, "What can I do for you? I can't ask you into the living room just now – the carpet's up and it's not fit to be seen."

Recalled to the purpose of her visit, Lady Courtney weighed in, "I'll come straight to the point then. I want your assurance that this unfortunate friendship between your nephew and my daughter will go no further. I'm sure you agree with me that the whole thing is quite absurd, and is not to be encouraged. I, for my part, will ensure my daughter will be given a good talking to, and will not be allowed to communicate with your nephew in future."

Bristling, Aunt Ethel stiffened at the announcement. "I shall do no such thing. My nephew is old enough to decide such matters for himself, without any interference on my part – or anyone else's," she added pointedly.

"But my good woman," argued Lady Courtney earnestly, beginning to see her task was not as easy as she had supposed. "Surely you can see how unrealistic the whole matter is, from everyone's point of view. Let's face it, our daughter Sally is the daughter of a knight of the realm and your nephew is what – an unpaid assistant in the village shop. Need I say more?"

"I thought your ladyship was a believer in social justice and equal rights?" said Aunt Ethel folding her arms, prepared to do battle.

Affronted, Lady Courtney drew herself up. "As you know very well, I have been a lifelong supporter of equal rights for many years. I fail to see what that has to do with the case in point. Besides," she pointed out icily, changing her attack, "it's not just a matter of one's station in life – which is immaterial, as far as I am concerned - it's a question of honour and moral character. And I believe you know what I am referring to."

"I have no idea, but I am sure you are going to tell me," sniffed Aunt Ethel.

"Over the past weeks, my husband and I have been extremely upset and outraged at the way your nephew has been toying with my gel's affections, when all the time he has been acting in a disgraceful way, doing his best to lead that poor innocent girl astray when she has come to this country, expecting to be treated with courtesy and consideration - not by the unwelcome attention of philanderers."

"If you're talking about that girl, Veronica," retorted Aunt Ethel sharply, "I understand she's been chasing him ever since she got here, and hasn't given him a moment's peace."

"Well, if that's your attitude, I don't think there is anything more to say," Lady Courtney said stiffly, turning to go.

"Although they do say she's got her eye on that boy of yours," added Aunt Ethel carelessly, dusting a vase.

"What-what was that you said?" asked Lady Courtney electrified. "Do you mean Lancelot? Who-who told you that?"

"Why William phoned me a few minutes before you arrived. He says that Lance of yours has proposed to Veronica and she's accepted – and the old man's given his approval, so I presume that makes it official."

Lady Courtney tottered, and reached out for the nearest table for support. "Why, if that's true, it puts an entirely different complexion on things."

"They say her old man's loaded as well, so that can't be bad, can it?" Aunt Ethel reminded her.

"Oh, my God! And I told him I forbade the marriage!" Lady Courtney was all of a twitter. "I hope he didn't think…I must go, if you'll excuse me. Oh, dear, what can I say?"

"You could tell him you were so delighted about the proposal that you wanted to postpone Sally's wedding so they could both get married at the same time," suggested Aunt Ethel helpfully.

Flustered, Lady Courtney gave a hunted look and moaned. "I must go, thank you for letting me know. I hope I'm not too late. What will Ed-ward think?"

Aunt Ethel closed the door and looked thoughtful. Her visitor's lavish praise of equal rights and the suffragette movement had given her an idea. Picking up the wiping up cloth she inspected it closely, then catching sight of a family nativity picture gazing down at her sternly, she turned it to the wall with a hasty apology, before reaching out for the scissors and proceeding to cut out the cheery greeting on the cloth inscribed 'Welcome to Snuggleton-near-the-Sea'. Gazing critically at her handiwork, the ragged edges did not seem quite right so she rubbed one of her muddy garden shoes over the cloth to give it the appearance of age. As an afterthought, she added an old photograph to the collection showing her in a group shot as a girl guide, and wrapping them up carefully together she put on her hat and coat and hurried out after her visitor.

Back in the shop, an atmosphere of bewilderment still reigned until the sudden arrival of Sally diverted their attention.

With a glad cry, Sally threw herself in William's arms.

"Oh, darling, I'm so glad I got here in time, I beat Ma to it."

"No, she's been and gone," he reassured her. "She's having it out with Aunt Ethel. I don't know who'll come out worse."

There was a cough in the background and Ed stepped forward, a dazed look on his face. "Say, pardon me for mentioning, but am I to understand that you and he are that way?"

William just had time to nod confirmation before being enveloped in Sally's arms again, accompanied by sighs of bliss.

A look of intense relief spread over Ed's face, and he dug William playfully in the ribs. "Why, you sly old dog you. There was I having the heebie-jeebies, wondering how to break the news about Vee, and all the time you were already fixed up with Miss Sally here."

There was a yelp of pleasure from Lance as he added his congratulations. "I say, Sis, this calls for a celebration. I had no idea."

In the middle of this happy scene of mutual congratulations, Lady Courtney chose to make her entrance, panting with the effort of getting there, in a headlong rush to make her apologies.

"Hey, Margery, you look all spooked out," cried Ed, concerned at the state of his old friend. "What's wrong?"

"Oh, Ed-ward, I don't know how to apologise for my dreadful rudeness just now – I don't know what came over me. I hardly know what to say."

"Why, Margery, you don't have to explain."

"But I do, I do," she burst out feverishly. "When I said I forbade the marriage, I wasn't talking about dear Veronica." She went on defensively. "I'm absolutely delighted to hear the news about her and Lance, absolutely thrilled!"

"Then what's the beef then?" enquired Ed, puzzled. "You certainly threw a wobbly back there."

"Yes, what were you getting at?" asked Lance. "I thought you'd be pleased."

"Oh, I am, you don't know how glad I am to welcome your dear daughter into our family."

"Then why?" repeated Lance, gathering courage. "I thought for a moment something terrible had happened."

Lady Courtney looked cornered. "Well, if you must know, I thought you were talking about William here."

Ed looked shocked. "You mean my fine young friend Willie, here, who single-handedly got rid of that crook Foxey - who wanted to ruin this lovely village of yours, and nearly got away with all my savings into the bargain?"

"Well, er, there were other reasons." She licked her lips.

"And who I'm appointing as my new manager in recognition of his sterling qualities of enterprise and initiative?" continued Ed unchecked.

"Oh darling!" cried Sally enthusiastically. "Now we can afford to get married."

She turned to Lance who whispered in her ear, and wheeled back, her face radiant. "And guess what, darling? Lance wants to publish those stories of yours."

"What?" exclaimed Lady Courtney, taken aback. "I didn't know you worked for a publisher?" as if she was seeing him for the first time in a new light.

Lance shuffled his feet. "I didn't want to tell you, Ma, until they decided to take me on permanently. I've got a sort of roving commission, on the lookout for new talent, don't you know."

There was an unexpected interruption as the shop door opened again, admitting Aunt Ethel.

"Look who I found outside!" greeted Aunt Ethel, pulling someone in behind her.

"Er, hello, m'dear," acknowledged Sir Henry, looking embarrassed. "The door seemed to have got stuck or something."

"Oh, there you are, dear." Lady Courtney heaved a sigh of heartfelt relief. "You're just in time to hear some exciting news. Your dear boy, Lance, here, is going to marry Veronica – isn't that wonderful?"

"Wonderful," gasped Sir Henry, not quite sure if he heard properly. "You don't mean our Sally and er, young William, then?"

"No, of course not," corrected his wife, rallying. "I was just explaining..."

"Excuse me, Lady Courtney," butted in Aunt Ethel, before the discussion got any further complicated.

"Yes, what is it?" Her intervention was almost greeted with open arms.

"Well," began Aunt Ethel diffidently, "knowing how interested you are in the suffragette movement, I thought you might like to see these old family heirlooms I came across by accident."

"Lady Courtney gave a dismissive glance at the collection. "I fail to see what it has to do with what we were talking about."

"You'd be surprised," replied Aunt Ethel helpfully. "I was going to say my grandmother was a close friend of one of the pioneers of the movement, and went on all those hunger strikes, but perhaps that wouldn't interest you?"

Lady Courtney's eyes opened wide with awe, and she clutched her arm, "What are you saying? You mean, you're one of us?"

"That's right," agreed Aunt Ethel, crossing her fingers, and telling herself it was all for a good cause. "Many's the time I've heard of the scrapes they got into. Oh, and I thought you might be interested in some of the little treasures she left me. This is a photo showing us all together at a reunion." She held up the picture of her Girl Guide group. "And this," she presented the soiled washing up towel with a flourish. "You'll never guess what this is."

"What?" whispered Lady Courtney eagerly, hanging on every word.

"Some say this could be the very cloth they used to wash their feet after the hunger march."

"No," breathed her enthralled listener. Her voice trembled. "May I...am I permitted to touch it?"

"Yes, just this once. I have to be careful it doesn't get spoiled, otherwise it loses its special condition."

"Yes, yes, I quite see that." She touched it reverently. "I don't suppose you would consider lending it for a special display I was planning for the Women's Forum?"

"Well, seeing as it's you, your Ladyship – I'd have to be in charge of it, of course."

"Of course, and naturally I would give you full recognition."

"I'm glad that's settled," Lance interrupted pointedly, on prompting from Sally. "You were just going to tell us why you wanted to put a stop to Sally's wedding plans."

"I-I er," Lady Courtney looked around, trapped. Suddenly catching sight of Aunt Ethel making signals, she remembered her tongue-in-cheek suggestion, and announced shakily, "Why, I er, of course, I wanted to make sure it didn't clash with dear Lance and Veronica's plans, naturally." Her voice gathered confidence. "I was only thinking of those two, what else?"

"Then I can think of an even better idea," beamed Sir Henry, starting to revive like a watered flower at the thought of such a magic solution to restoring the family fortunes. "Why don't we make it a double wedding? That's the ticket, what?"

"Why, gee, that's great," approved Ed, beaming. "This calls for a celebration. "Get the glasses out, Willie."

"Does anyone know what's happened to Vee?" asked Lance plaintively, as they waited.

On cue, the door swung open, and Veronica stood there heaving mutinously. "Say, what's going on in here? Am I supposed to wait all night before I can join in?"

Ed looked guilty. "Gee, I'm sorry, Vee honey, we've just been hearing all the good news about Willie and Sally here. Isn't that just great?"

At the sight of William holding Sally close, all her old feelings about him re-surfaced and she swayed towards him. "Since when this has been going on, Willie - I thought you and me were buddy boys?"

It was clear from her tone of voice that getting bored with all the waiting, she had already started celebrating on her own.

While everyone watched hypnotised, William cleared his throat and said soothingly, "Of course we are, Vee. Like you are with Lance – he's over there," as if making the situation quite clear.

"You don't say – Lance is my old buddy boy too," she focused her eyes in his direction.

From the other side of the room, Lance stepped forward hopefully. At the sight of him, flanked by Lady Courtney and Sir Henry, a vision of the future linked to Lancelot began to claim her attention, and the image of him was replaced by a servant bowing before her and announcing respectfully, "Dinner is served, your Ladyship."

Her vision faded and Veronica smiled, all her doubts resolved. "Coming, Lance, darling."

The tension broken, William gulped with relief and Lady Courtney and Sir Henry breathed freely again, holding out their arms as if they were in sight of the promised land.

Wiping his brow, Ed felt the urgent need for fresh air and for something far stronger than anything the shop had available in emergencies such as these.

"Excuse me folks, I'll be right back in two shakes – you carry on without me."

Before anyone could object, he slipped out of the side door, searching feverishly in his pocket for a slip of paper as he went, and read the message it held in the manner of one of King Arthur's Knights going into battle. He repeated the instructions reverently to himself as it instructed him to 'Knock twice and ask for a dose of Ferdie's medicine', and carefully replacing the note began skipping along the high street, humming to himself happily.

* * *

If you enjoyed this book please take the time to leave a review. It would mean a lot to me.
And check out my other books on my website:
http://www.michaelwilton.co.uk/
and from my page at Next Chapter:
https://www.nextchapter.pub/authors/michael-n-wilton
The story continues in *In The Soup.*
https://www.nextchapter.pub/books/in-the-soup

About The Author

Following National Service in the RAF Michael returned to banking, until an opportunity arose to pursue a career in writing. After working as a press officer for several electrical engineering companies, he was asked to set up a central press office as a group press officer for an engineering company. From there he moved on to become publicity manager for a fixed wing and helicopter charter company, where he was involved in making a film of the company's activities at home and overseas.

He became so interested in filming that he joined up with a partner to make industrial films for several years, before ending his career handling research publicity for a national gas transmission company.

Since retiring he has fulfilled his dream of becoming a writer and has written two books for children as well as several romantic comedies.

You can read more about Michael on his website:
http://www.michaelwilton.co.uk/
Amazon:
https://www.amazon.co.uk/Michael-N.-Wilton/e/B00EPG3SF4

Save Our Shop
ISBN: 978-4-86751-324-8 (Large Print)

Published by
Next Chapter
1-60-20 Minami-Otsuka
170-0005 Toshima-Ku, Tokyo
+818035793528
2nd July 2021

Lightning Source UK Ltd.
Milton Keynes UK
UKHW010200070223
416581UK00003B/105